A CABOT CAIN THRILLER

ASSAULT ON AGATHON

Also from ALAN CAILLOU

<u>CABOT CAIN</u> Series
Assault on Kolchak
Assault on Ming
Assault on Loveless
Assault on Fellawi
Assault on Agathon
Assault on Aimata

<u>TOBIN'S WAR</u> Series
Dead Sea Submarine
Terror in Rio
Congo War Cry
Afghan Assault
Swamp War
Death Charge
The Garonsky Missile

<u>MIKE BENASQUE</u> Series
The Plotters
Marseilles
Who'll Buy My Evil
Diamonds Wild

<u>IAN QUAYLE</u> Series
A League of Hawks
The Swords of God

<u>DEKKER'S DEMONS</u> Series
Suicide Run
Blood Run

Rogue's Gambit
Cairo Cabal
Bichu the Jaguar
The Walls of Jolo
The Hot Sun of Africa
The Cheetahs
Joshua's People
Mindanao Pearl
Khartoum
South from Khartoum
Rampage
The World is 6 Feet Square
The Prophetess
House on Curzon Street

The Charge of the Light Brigade
A Journey to Orassia

CHAPTER 1

It has always seemed strange to me that it should be so easy to head into tomorrow's disasters with today's euphoric sense of well-being. Surely there should be some mechanism, some intellectual process that might say: *slow down, you're heading for trouble...*

But if there were—sometimes, avoiding trouble is more troublesome than meeting it head on. If I hadn't gone off to the mountains for a little peace and quiet, something I'm not very used to, who knows what would have happened to Fenrek?

And so, I was racing along the Riviera with nothing but the delights of the sun, of fresh air, of good food and wine in my mind, without even an inkling of all the terrors that were being enacted just a few miles away, over the border.

Even at speed, I could smell the sweet candy scent of the honeysuckle that trailed over the retaining walls, white stone interspersed with the glaring reds of bougainvillea and geranium, with the bright green shrubbery climbing up the mountain on my left and the cool blue of the sea, unbelievably cobalt-colored, down there below me on the right.

The Corniche is a good road, cutting through the mountain in long dark tunnels, and I held the Jensen to a steady eighty miles an hour, hugging the wide bends, and enjoying the exhilaration of the fresh sea wind; Miramare had never looked more lovely, with its white villas, tiled rooftops, and the beautiful trellised gardens with their casual grapevines giving an anticipatory edge to my appetite. A holiday, and the first I'd set out on in a long time.

Were they, at that moment, beating you to a pulp, Fenrek? Was that the moment when they brought out the hypodermic? Who could ever know?

Twelve kilometers from Trieste, I swung the wheel over into the dirt road, and slowed down to take the steep climb up to the old Hotel Monterosso, which is where I always stay when I'm anywhere in this charming stretch of the Adriatic. It's been there for just over five hundred years, though the two-storied red marble porch that runs along the side that faces the sea is considerably older—all that's left of the old Palace the Venetian Doge Domenico Michiel built on the top of the little mountain in the year 1127. And in one corner of the terrace, now the garden restaurant, there is a very striking statue carved by Donatello, the greatest of all the Florentine sculptors before Michelangelo. A half-nude pagan girl-child that was originally intended for his Prato Cathedral facade—but which somehow got left out of that Bacchanalian masterpiece—she stands on one lithe leg in the corner, ready to leap down into the sea that lies, at this point, eight hundred feet below. There is a sly, childish smile on her face and a weathered rose in her hand; and this statue alone is cause enough for anyone to brave the wretched, pot-holed track that leads to the hotel.

As I drove up and parked just below the red balustrade, the scent of flowers was gone, and there was instead the smell of braising *osso bucco*, ripe with fresh rosemary, coming from the kitchens.

The clerk said, beaming: "Ah, Mr. Cain, it's good to see you again. And a lady has been telephoning for you."

There was almost nobody who knew I'd be staying at the Monterosso, and when I asked, the clerk shrugged. "She would not leave her name, Mr. Cain, but she's been telephoning every hour on the hour since six o'clock this morning. Long distance. From Karlovac."

Karlovac...About a hundred and fifty kilometers over the border in Yugoslavia.

I looked at my watch; it was a quarter till one. I said: "Seven long distance calls, and she didn't leave a number?" I was trying to think who, among my friends, could possibly be in Karlovac.

The clerk was a plump and middle-aged man who lived, at

home, in a permanent state of terror of his wife and his eleven children; but here, in the stately quiet of the old hotel, he was gentle, efficient— and a barbarous disciplinarian. He said, smiling:

"The first call came from Valandovo, the second from Skopje, the third from somewhere on the road to Sarajevo, then from Sarajevo itself, and finally from Banya Luka."

"So whoever she is, she's on her way here, and driving this way fast by the sound of it."

"On those roads, very fast."

"Then save me a table for two for lunch, will you? About two o'clock?"

"Of course. We have *osso bucco* today."

"Yes. I can smell it. And if the lady calls at one, I'll be in my room. Do I have the same room?"

"Of course, Mr. Cain, as usual, thirty-seven."

"Good. Would you send me up some wine? Some of the Refosco, if you still have it."

He was beaming again, and I knew what he was thinking; the Monterosso has a small selection of Roman wine jugs, museum pieces all of them, immensely valuable, made of crude glass with a faint mauve tinge to it; and Refosce is a rare wine with a definite violet flush to it that gives the ancient glass a miraculous deep-blue color all its own; it's not the best wine in the world, but the combination of colors is irresistible.

He found a key and told one of the pages to bring out a Roman bottle, and said to him sharply: "And you handle it with great care, you understand? If it gets damaged, you know what will happen to you!" The thought appalled the page, and he visibly paled.

I went up to my room, looked around and noted that nothing had changed since my last visit. The big four-poster bed was ornate and gaudy, seventeenth century from Venice, with intricately-carved oak pillars. The work of an unknown craftsman at the Court of Fra Paolo Sarpi, the carving was overlaid in gilt and colored enamels, astonishingly brilliant; it always made me remember that it was the Venetians—who had no trees, no green fields, no gardens, no flowers (so they called sea shells *flor di mare*, 'flowers of the sea'), no orchards or forests, none of the acceptable colors of Nature itself except the grey of the water and the white of the Lido—who were the first painters to use color for its own sake. There were two beautiful Venetian chairs of carved walnut and red velvet, high backed, heavy, and comfortable, and a beautiful cabinet on a carved oak stand, decorated with exquisite floral marquetry; it seemed a shame to use such a cabinet for socks and underwear and shirts, but that's what it was there for.

At three minutes past one, while I was sipping the tart, almost sour wine and enjoying the eerie light that streamed through the bottle on the table by the window, the phone rang, and I felt a little tinge of excitement, because, thinking about it, I'd realized that there was only one person who could possibly know—or guess—that I might conceivably be here.

I heard, first, a sharp and angry exchange of female voices speaking Serbo-Croatian, one of them heavily accented; the accent was what? Greek? The line was bad, and someone was complaining about it angrily. The line cleared, and the Greek accent switched to English and asked: "Hullo? Monterosso? Well? Is he there, or isn't he?"

I said: "Cabot Cain here."

I heard her sharp intake of breath. "Mr. Cain?"

"Yes, indeed. How can I help you?"

I was right; it was Greek. She switched to her native tongue—whoever she was, at least she knew that much about me!—and said, very quickly: "I have to be cautious, I'm in great trouble, and that doesn't matter, but a mutual friend is in trouble too, and that does. Can you hear me?"

"Suppose you tell me your name."

She hesitated. Then: "Maria Christophorous, friend of...a very close friend of yours."

Ha! Maria Christophorous!

I said: "Yes; I know who you are, and I know whom you are talking about. Now tell me *where* you are. At the rate you're traveling, you should be somewhere around Postojna. I've ordered lunch for two o'clock, can you make it?"

I could almost visualize her shaking head. There was an apprehensive tone in her voice, and she said: "No, no I don't think I can. I'm near Postojna, in a village called Vipava, that's about thirty kilometers from where you are now, could you come here?"

"Yes. Yes, I could."

"You take the road to Postojna and branch off at..."

"I know where Vipava is. How will I find you there?"

"I won't be there. I'll be on the road between Vipava and Aidussina." Are you still driving the same car?' She said quickly, and quite unnecessarily: "Don't mention the make, but I want to know what to look for."

I sighed. "Yes, the same car."

"You know what a D 8-120 looks like?"

"My God, you mean a nineteen thirty-two Delage? Yes, I do."

"Look for one, a dark blue convertible, I must go now."

"Just tell me..."

She interrupted and there was a catch in her voice, not quite crying but very close to it. She said: "Please, please, Mr. Cain. For God's sake. Hurry,"

She rang off.

A magpie was sitting on the window ledge, fascinated by the purple of the wine bottle; I moved it to a safer place and went downstairs to find the Jensen. I took off at high speed down the snaking track that led to the Corniche once again, made a left turn and another left onto the side road that leads to the tiny sleepy frontier post at Bistja—the sleepier they are, the better, if you're in a hurry; it is a likelihood that the larger posts have lines of cars waiting for the inevitable close scrutiny. I was worried about the visa problem, but American passports are very welcome in Yugoslavia these days, and I guessed, correctly, that the problem would not be insurmountable.

It wasn't. The guard was courteous, stern and very correct, but there were provisions for such emergencies. I was able to obtain a visa right there, and it only took a few minutes until I was pushing the Jensen again along the narrow, winding road that led through the beautiful forest of grey and green hazel trees, with ice-cold streams tumbling down from the high mountains, and a silence in which even the refined purr of the engine seemed obtrusive, soft and soothing as it was. Less than ten miles from the noisy bustle of Trieste and the coastal ports, the countryside was as rural and lovely as any I have ever seen. The air was clean and inviting, the trees were fragrant. There was no traffic at all; after the crowded roads of Italy, it made a very pleasant change.

Twenty minutes after the telephone call, I was passing through a tiny collection of wooden houses, steeply roofed against the winter snow, where a signpost set at a crazy angle in the dirt road said: "VIPAVA 1 KM. ADJOVSCINA 8 KMs."

Aidussina, she had called it, the old Italian name in this much-disputed territory; I swung the wheel over and started looking out for a 1932 Delage, one of the truly great cars of history, slowing down now to little more than a crawl, keeping the speedo-needle below the sixty mark all the time.

I found the car parked just off the road, under a thick clump of clematis that was straggling brightly over the rocks. Parked is not quite the right word, and neither is hidden; it had been carefully squeezed in among the shrubbery and the boulders, more than half out of sight and only visible if you were actually looking for it. The fear that had been in her voice made me take certain precautions, and I drove past it slowly for a mile, then came back and parked nearby to watch it for a few moments. The top was down, and there was nobody in it.

Nobody in it.

I stopped the Jensen and switched off, and walked over to see what there was to see. Somehow I was not surprised to see a clumsy-looking bundle lying in the back, half on the floor and half on the seat, covered with a very expensive mohair car rug, one of the old-fashioned kind that went very well with this kind of car.

And the Delage! It was a beauty, an early model built just after Delage was bought out by Delahaye in the thirties, long and low and svelte, with a louvered hood and huge Marchal headlights, its body perfect under a heavy coat of road dust, its leather and woodwork immaculate; someone was spending a lot of money to keep this fabulous machine the way it should be kept. I badly wanted to press the starter and hear it whisper to me, but I thought I'd better not touch anything, not with a body in the back and three neat round bullet holes in the car's bodywork. High-velocity rifle by the look of them, but it's not always possible to tell. No way to treat a fabulous car like this, in any case.

I took a good look around to make sure I was alone, and then went to look at the body in the back.

Thank God it wasn't my mysterious caller.

It was a man, small and dark and wiry, an East European by the looks of him, perhaps a Bulgarian. The tight jacket was of pure but low-grade wool, with wide short lapels and a dark stripe; the cuffs were just on the verge of fraying, proclaiming the kind of respectable poverty of certain Eastern countries. Black, thin-soled shoes, as dusty as the car's polish, and socks with a red-and-white design running up the sides of them. The tie was Italian, from a discount store in Milan, and the shirt was heavy and also made of low-grade wool. He had a neat black moustache, long sideburns, a two-day growth of beard, and a small round bole just above his left ear that looked as if it had come from a .22. The body was cold, and had begun to stiffen. His pockets were quite empty. I was wondering about the indelible blue stain on his lips when there was a flash of light half behind me and I dove to the ground to wait for the sound of the shot; it didn't come, and when, feeling a little foolish, I got to my feet again, there was the light once more, a helio, someone signaling with a mirror, out of her purse no doubt. I covered up the body again and went to see who she was.

Just across the road, up the steep slope and in among the green and silent trees, it's cool and friendly and sweet smelling. A lot of pines here, with a broad grass-covered clearing that made a small cliff top overlooking the buff-colored pebbles of the road. I saw her when I reached the top, a slight, black-haired woman wearing dark glasses, dressed in white linen pants and a red sweater. She tucked her mirror back into her purse and hurried towards me, coming out of the trees and looking carefully back over her shoulder. A twig caught in her open-toed sandals and she kicked it away impatiently, scowling and sort of jumping to keep her balance, a lively, energetic young woman of thirty or so. She had a small, expensive traveling case slung over her shoulder, the sort of woman who won't even go to the can without a change of clothing handy.

She was half-running, half-walking, and she didn't wait until she got where she was going before she started talking urgently, in rapid and fluent and accented English, the words all tumbling out, without pause, as though there were no time to say all that had to be said, all very brisk and businesslike.

"Mr. Cain? I'm glad you got here so soon, do you have a camera with you? We have to take that man's picture and then get him the hell out of my car, he's already been bleeding all over my car rug."

She shot out her hand and took mine and said politely, smiling: "So good of you to come, I knew you would. Don't you always carry a camera with you? From what I've heard I'd say you were the sort of man who does." She was still holding onto my hand, looking up at me and trying not to be surprised by my size; I'm six feet seven and weigh a mite over two hundred pounds, and it throws people sometimes. But she knew, of course, she'd heard all about me. She said quickly, not waiting for anything: "I'm Maria Christophorous, of course, but do you know anything more than that? Our mutual friend..."

Maybe she was conscious that I was waiting for the verbiage to come to an end, because she stopped abruptly and suddenly pulled off her dark glasses. Her eyes were good sized and black, a trifle too made-up; perhaps it showed more because she'd been crying.

I said: "You told me on the phone that he was in trouble. Are we talking about the Colonel?"

"Yes. About Mat Fenrek. He's been kidnapped."

"Oh."

It didn't seem to me a very likely thing to happen, and I didn't immediately believe it. Colonel Matthias Fenrek, an old and dear friend, was head of Interpol's B7 Department, and not the kind of man to run into that sort of trouble at all—or any other trouble that he couldn't handle, either.

I said: "Suppose we get down to my car and drive off somewhere just in case someone should happen along and spot the Delage? Who's the passenger, incidentally?"

"I don't know, that's why we have to photograph him. I've schlepped him over half the country. I've got his fingerprints, of course, but we need a photograph as well: You *do* have a camera, don't you? If not...Oh, my God, if you haven't, we'll have to drive up to Ljubljana and buy one, that's why I couldn't cross the border, the frontier guards are fussy about that sort of thing..."

She went on and on, and I waited for the energy to dry up, and at last she broke off and asked brightly: "Am I talking too much?"

I said: "Uh-huh."

"Oh." She looked abashed for a moment; and then continued: "Well, I got his fingerprints, of course, and a PP as well, but I thought a photograph would help too."

PP stands for Portrait Parle, the invention of Alphonse Bertillon, the first man to apply anthropometry to criminal investigation; *Bertillonage*, as it's usually called, means identification by means of meticulous body measurements.

I said: "Suppose you tell me what Fenrek is doing in Yugoslavia to start with. I haven't seen him for a couple of months."

On the road below us a truck went hurtling by, rattling and sending up a cloud of yellow dust. Maria pulled back under cover, pulling me unnecessarily with her as she did so. She moved with a peculiarly smooth, effortless sort of muscular control that was quite astonishing to watch, as though no conscious exertion were needed, her body gliding. Her eyes seemed always to be on mine, as though seeking out on my face all the answers to history; hers were dark and lively eyes, quite beautifully expressive. I recalled that this was one of Mat Fenrek's weaknesses: a pair of eyes like that could make a lovesick schoolboy out of him in no time at all.

Staring at me, she said: "Well, he was investigating a bank robbery, a series of bank robberies, and it wasn't only in Yugoslavia either, it was first in Greece and then in..." She broke off and stared at me. I stared back a look of question, and she said slowly: "When I said that, a veil dropped over your eyes. You really *are* Cabot Cain, aren't you? Yes, of course, you couldn't very well be anybody else, could you? You do tend to stand out a bit, don't you? Why did you query what I was saying?"

I said: "I didn't open my mouth."

"What did I say that made you stop and think?"

"I never have to stop to think."

"No, but...What was it?"

"Fenrek investigating a bank robbery? He's on the Staff, not a Field Operative."

"Yes, I know that. But that's what he was doing, none the less." She kept on staring at me. "And you don't think it makes sense."

"If that's what he was doing, it makes sense. But he's still not the kind of man to get himself into trouble of that nature."

"No, but his office is the kind that invites trouble, isn't it?"

"He's an executive, a comfortable desk in Paris! No one would dare to kidnap him, to begin with."

"Oh, nonsense!"

"There are some people who just naturally get themselves into trouble, and some who just naturally stay out of it. Fenrek belongs in the latter category, emphatically."

"Well, be that as it may, they dared, and they did it. And why are we standing here doing nothing, when so much has to be done?"

I said: "*They* did it? Who's *they?*"

She said, with a great deal of impatience: "That's what we've got to find out, isn't it?"

I fancied I could hear the soft motor of a good car further down the road, moving quite slowly; or was it only a trick played by the wind among the trees, the sound of running water? She hadn't heard it, and I said: "A car there somewhere."

She froze, a study in arrested motion, and listened. She said at last, whispering all the same: "No, it's the wind, it plays tricks in the hills."

"A car. A mile or two up the road. This is the only road there is around here."

She shook her head again and said, still whispering: "The first thing, we've got to get some photographs of the dead man, then we'll find a way to get rid of the body."

"How did he get to be bleeding all over your car?"

"Oh. Well, he was taking shots at me with a rifle, you saw the bullet holes in the car. I saw you looking at them."

"Go on."

"And so, I shot him."

"At close range, with a pistol."

"Yes. I stalked him in the woods until I got close enough." She pulled back the sleeve of her sweater and showed me the blood-stained white handkerchief around her forearm. She said calmly: "This was at close range too, but I got my shot in first and so his was not too effective."

I said: "What's that blue stain on his lips?"

She frowned, her dark brows coming together; it made her

look almost Satanic. "Blue stain? I didn't notice it. Can we get on with what we have to do?"

I sighed and took her elbow and guided her down the slope to the road. We stopped by the Jensen, and I took the Honeywell Pentax from the glove compartment. We walked together over to the hidden Delage, pushing our way through the overhanging trees.

Even before we reached the car, I saw that he was no longer there. From up where my head is, the view is better, and I put a hand behind her and shoved hard, and threw myself after her into the bushes, and it was only just in time. The swathe of bullets whipped through the trees over our heads, a Bren gun by the sound of it, and I fell on top of Maria and dragged her closer under cover, rolling over and over with her until we reached a ditch in the forest floor, lined with wet leaves and smelling of autumn. I grabbed her wrist and whispered: "This way, quickly," and we half-ran, half-crawled, in the direction of the gunfire.

Then I heard a car start up, a little to our left, round a bend in the narrow forest-fringed road, and I peered through the leaves and saw it there, a pale-grey Citroen station wagon, and two men were just getting into it, a third starting it up. As I watched, it took off fast, and we stayed under cover as it raced past my Jensen, narrowly missing the offside wing, and one of the men shoved his arm through the window and threw a hand grenade. I gasped as it bounced on the Jensen's hood and dropped to the road, rolled on and on into the bushes, and came to rest against the left rear wheel of the Delage. I couldn't help wincing.

I shoved Maria into the ground and fell on top of her, her tiny body hidden completely underneath me, but soft and resilient and somehow deserving of a better posture.

The grenade went off, and was followed by another, fiercer burst as the Delage's gas tank blew up. A great sheet of red and yellow flame shot out among the fresh green trees, and she wailed: "Oh no, my beautiful car..."

I said, a trifle unkindly: "It could have been worse. That was meant for the Jensen." She looked at me in absolute horror.

I took her arm again. "It seems they've gone, and at least we don't have the problem of disposing of a dead man. Why don't we go back across the border and have some lunch? Do you have a passport?"

"Yes."

"Any other problems that might preclude your crossing over the border?"

"No. There was just that body."

"So let's go."

The Delage was a smoldering wreck, the black smoke staining the scenery, and she stared at it and almost wept. "It was a Saoutchik body, I'll never be able to replace it, never!"

I said gently: "Why don't we go back to the Monterosso and do some talking. We've got to find Mat Fenrek, remember?"

She said: "Then what are we standing here for like a couple of idiots?"

We got into the Jensen, drove back to the Monterosso, and I took her to my room to show her the purple wine in its violet amphora, and one hour late for our two o'clock lunch, we sat down in the little terrace garden, close by Donatello's little pagan nymph, and ate *osse bucco* together.

Maria had freshened up in my bathroom and shaken out her shining ebony hair. And I'd been quite wrong when I'd put her at thirty. Looking very closely, I saw that she was a lot older. A splendid smooth skin, not a wrinkle to be seen, a teenager's figure as lithe and taut and delightful as any California surfer's, but none the less well into her forties.

It was in her manner more than in her looks, and if she'd insisted she was twenty, I'd almost have believed her.

CHAPTER 2

She said, looking around in admiration: "So this is the famous hideaway. That's what the Colonel called it, he said: 'If Cain's anywhere in these parts he'll be at the Monterosso, we must go and look him up there when all this is over, ruin his holiday for him.'"

She was toying with the salad, picking out the little cloves of garlic and nibbling on them, and I said: "What does 'all this' mean? I'm damn sure there's more to it than bank robberies,"

I studied her now, fascinated by a strange sort of secrecy about her, as though under the surface some very recondite force was driving her. She used lavish gestures when she talked, waving her hands around; it was almost as if she wanted to show them off, hands that were delicately made and white as marble. She wore no rings, but a single heavy bracelet of polished gold wires, bound around an oblong watch that had a rutilated quartz crystal; here and there, tiny diamonds had been set among the gold wires, and I thought it must have been made by Andrew Grima in London, an exquisite piece of avant-garde jewelry, designed with great imagination and executed with masterly craftsmanship.

She said firmly: "Bank robberies. One in Larissa, another in Paloviv, and a third in Skopje."

I said: "Greece, Bulgaria, and Yugoslavia, and they all, presumably, had something in common."

"This salad is delicious. Is that rosemary or oregano?"

"Neither. It's *Majorana onites*, or pot marjoram if you prefer that."

"Do you think they'd give me some recipes if I asked them nicely?"

"What did the three bank robberies have in common?"

"Well, in each case, two heavily armed men—machine guns and hand grenades—entered the bank, while four others guarded the approaches. They arrived and left in pairs, using three stolen cars. Each robbery was timed with an admirable military precision."

"And the proceeds?"

"Heavy, in all three. Shipments of currency had just arrived. A rough quarter of a million dollars, in your currency equivalent, every time."

"Well, Bulgaria is not a subscriber to Interpol, but Greece and Yugoslavia are, and if one of those two Police Departments asked for Interpol help—yes, they'd be interested. But it just isn't Fenrek's job to go around investigating things for himself. Not that kind of trivia, anyway."

"But that's what he was doing. What am I going to do about my beautiful Delage?"

I shrugged. "What can you do? It's a burned-out wreck. All you can do is forget it."

"Maybe I'll get a Jensen."

"Tell me about the kidnapping."

She frowned, but only because she couldn't find any more garlic cloves in the salad. Where, I wondered, were the tears I had almost heard on the telephone? I thought I'd better ask her, so I said:

"You don't believe he's in any great danger, do you? And yet, when you called me, you were very close to...shall I call it hysteria? What happened in between?"

She did not take her eyes off her plate, and she waited a little while before answering. Then she said at last, very quietly, and without all that rush of words that was her hallmark:

"When I called first, at six in the morning; they said you were coming but didn't know when. And I called and called, and called, and finally...Well, I almost gave you up. And I was quite alone, can you understand that? But now, now I'm not alone any more, and even if I don't know what to do, you will." She looked up at me suddenly, and now her eyes were wet. She said: "Can you understand that? All I knew then was that he was in trouble and there was no one to help him. But now all that's changed, hasn't it?"

"So you've changed, too."

"Yes. I'm not...hysterical anymore. Now I know that something is going to be done."

The air was heavy with the mystic scent of verbena; there were great blue patches of it along the broken stone walls of the terrace, matching their brilliance against the deep blue of the Adriatic Sea. She looked out across the water now, and said: "We were in Skopje together, working on this case."

"Go back further."

"Oh. Well, the Colonel turned up in Athens, which is where I live, and I was helping him with his investigation."

I said carefully: "Whatever he's told you about me—you should know that I'm not an Interpol man. I'm not even supposed to know that he is. It's just that, very unofficially, I sometimes help him out."

She said airily: "Yes, I know that."

"Good. And you are, I believe, his representative in Greece. Or one of them."

"The only one."

A little discretion was needed. Fenrek has no weaknesses at all, but none the less, he has a girl tucked away in almost every major city on the face of the earth, and each thinks herself to be the one and only true love. He says it helps his work very considerably, and that makes it all correct and proper.

She said: "Field Representative, Grade 4A, yes, I take care of things there for him."

"And your cover?"

She shrugged. "I have no work, a lady of leisure. Each of my three husbands was a wealthy man."

"Three of them?"

"A widow three times, Mr. Cain. Two shipping magnates and one industrialist, and they all worked themselves into early graves and left me all their fortunes."

"It doesn't seem to worry you very much."

Again, that oh-so-elegant shrug. She looked at me calmly for a little while, and then said: "Now I have Fenrek. It makes up for everything."

"I see. So he turned up in Athens, and..."

"He was looking into this bank robbery in Larissa." She said, insisting: "Yes, he really was. One of the robbers was a man named Agathon, apparently, and that seemed enormously important to him, though he didn't tell me why. You know how he is."

"I do indeed."

"He found a contact, the son of a man just being released from prison in Italy."

"Named?"

"The son calls himself Jablanica, and drives a truck between Athens and Belgrade for a living, but he's really an Italian, and the family name is not Jablanica at all, but Giabianco, and his father, Vito Giabianco, is just finishing off five years in jail in Trieste for smuggling cigarettes and salt. Sentenced to five years, and that's what he served, no remission at all. He is supposed to know something of interest to Fenrek, though I have no idea what it is. Anyway, we were driving to Trieste, and that's when he told me you might be near there, at the Monterosso, and when we got to Valandovo, which is, what— thirty kilometers over the border from Greece?—he told the frontier police that a car had been following us all the way from Athens."

"Had you seen it?"

She hesitated. "Not really. I saw him looking rather strangely at a Citroen station wagon that was behind us at a railway crossing on the Greek side of the border, but that was the only time I saw it."

"The same station wagon that demolished your Delage?"

"Yes, and I wish you wouldn't rub that in, I'd rather forget all about it."

"Go on."

"Anyway, about fifty kilometers further on, just the other side of a village called Gradsko, he stopped the car, got out, told me to drive on to Skopje and tell the police there to put out a net for the Citroen, and for them to take it easy if there was any shooting because he would be in it. He didn't want any trigger-happy cops blasting away at it, because he was just taking a friendly little ride. He wanted it followed, as discreetly as possible, to see where it was going, where they were taking him."

"A risky business. You let him get away with it?"

She spread her hands wide, gesticulating as wildly as Fenrek does; I wondered if she'd picked it up from him, or if it was something they had in common. Nothing like the little physical similarities to bring the boys and the girls together.

Searching for the right phrases, she said: "But he's my commanding officer, Mr. Cain! Of course I objected, but you know you can't argue with him! He just smiled and said: 'There's no danger at all, just do as I tell you.' And he walked off and left me there. When I drove off, he was standing by the side of the road and...waiting."

I said: "What sort of shape was the Delage in?"

She was surprised. "Does that matter?"

"Of course. A question of one car catching another. The Citroen we saw was a Pallas, top speed around a hundred and twenty miles an hour. Could you better that in the Delage?"

She shook her head. "Thirty years ago, perhaps, but not anymore."

"Thirty years ago, the Delage was good for just over the hundred, which was considered a good speed in those days. Fenrek must have known that if it came to a race on the road to Trieste, which is usually deserted and goes on and on through the forests for a couple of hundred miles, you didn't have a hope in hell of getting away from them."

She frowned, and the tears were almost there again "That's what I came to realize. He was throwing himself to them to make sure they wouldn't get me as well. That's when I started calling you."

"You told the police in Skopje?"

"Yes, of course."

"But they got through the net, because we saw them. And there were three men with the car, no sign of Fenrek."

She'd been on the upgrade now that help was on its way, and now I'd started to ease her down again; she was trembling a little.

I said gently: "You see how we're slowly getting somewhere? Now at least we know that they dropped him off somewhere between Gradsko and where we saw them, near Postojna."

"But that's more than six hundred miles!"

"Five hundred and eighty to be precise. But it's already narrowing the field, and we'll narrow it down more, won't we? Tell me about your late passenger, the Bulgarian with the blue lips."

"Oh. Well, I was about twenty-five kilometers this side of Sarajevo, heading north to find you, and driving quite slowly because the road is very bad there. A couple of shots were fired at me. I realized by then that they—whoever they may be—had a faster car. It was no good trying to run for it, so I stopped and took cover in the forest, and that's when I saw him—one man with a rifle. He was about a hundred meters or so above me, crossing over to a better point of vantage, so I began to stalk him. He was stalking me, too, and we met halfway up the slope, and I got my shot in first, it's as simple as that."

Grade 4A, she'd be a crack shot, and would have graduated from the intense survival courses the B7 field operatives take, but there was a minor point I wanted to clear up. I said: "Are you damned good, or was he damned bad? It's a question of estimating the potential of the opposition."

"He was good. I'm better."

"Go on."

"Fenrek had the camera in his pocket, the little Minox, so I took his fingerprints and lugged him into the back of the car so that later I could get you to photograph his face. I used a ballpoint pen and a piece of notepaper for the fingerprints, and they really aren't as good as they should have been, so I thought that if we could send Special Index a PP and a couple of good photographs they'd have more to go on. He could have had a dozen aliases, half of them not fingerprinted, and a PP would have been very useful. And a mug shot."

It was an idiom she must have picked up from Fenrek. He doesn't realize the limits of his English, which is impeccable except when it comes to idiom; he always calls it "moog shot"; and she said it in exactly the same way; it sounded quite charming.

"So while I was safely out of the way up on the hillside with you, they sneaked in and recovered the body."

"Yes. And I do talk too much, don't I?"

"Much too much."

"That's what Fenrek says."

"And what Fenrek says is nearly always right."

"*Always* right."

"Uh-huh."

"And what do we do now?" She suddenly didn't want to eat any more, anxious to get going, and she pushed her plate away and said irritably: "And here we are sitting down and eating gorgonzola, hadn't we better...well, do something?"

"Such as?"

She waved her lovely hands at me again. "I don't know. Just...*something!*"

I said: "They won't push their luck for much longer in the Citroen. Even if they don't realize you must have alerted the police at Skopje—and I'm sure they do—they can be damn sure that their attack on us is going to be reported, so they must also be sure they can hide out not too far away. I won't believe they're going to drive five or six hundred miles in a wanted car, not in a country as well policed as this one is."

"They could change cars, of course. Steal another one, or have another one waiting."

"Quite possible. The best thing we can do is follow the only lead Fenrek's given us, and work back from Trieste. Vito Giabianco, do you have his address?"

She was already fumbling in her purse, and she brought out a slip of paper with some scribbling on it, and I said, with a touch of surprise: "You are not carrying it around with you written down, are you?"

She said firmly: "Yes, Mr. Cain, I am." She handed it to me and I apologized. It was Pitman's shorthand, transcribed from Italian into Greek, and finally into Pitman's with an admixture of Gregg's. She said, challenging me: "Safe enough?"

"No. Far too intriguing. They'd have made you decipher it."

"Oh. Well, there it is. Give it to me, I'll translate it for you."

I said: "Don't bother. Eighteen, Steps of the Virgin, Trieste, just off the Corso Veneta."

She was smiling faintly when she took the note back, and she had the grace to say nothing while she lit it with a slim platinum lighter and ground the residue to nothing in the ashtray. She said at last, softly:

"There, now it's safe."

"So let's go and see Vito Giabianco. Is he out already?"

She looked at the little Grima watch. "By the time we get there he will be. He's due for release at six this evening."

"And the house on the Virgin's Steps?"

"According to his son, it's been empty all these years. But an uncle had just moved in to get it ready for him, another Giabianco, this one from Turin."

There was a bell ringing at the back of my mind, and as I listened to if, it was no longer a bell but a piano, and the sound of it rang another bell, a Turkish note. It was clamoring to be heard, and then it all fell into place suddenly, as memories will.

I said: "Giabianco is not a very common name. Have you heard of Leonardo Giabianco?"

She shook her head. "Should I?"

"You're probably too young. What's your taste in music?"

"The moderns. Bartok, Copeland..."

"Oh my God. Anyway, Leonardo Giabianco was one of the greatest Mozart interpreters of all time. You might conceivably have heard his recordings, though they're all out of print now, the old seventy-eight rpms. I heard him play the Sonata in A Major once, and the third movement..."

"Ah yes, the Rondo alla Turka."

"It was marvelous. If I remember rightly, Leonardo had four or five sons, all of them musicians except one. And that one was the black sheep of the family, always in trouble with the police."

Her black eyes were wide. "Why, will it help us?"

"Yes. It'll give us a bond. Friend of a friend of a friend, many times removed, but still, a bond. The old man died a long time ago, but his name was magic in those days. And magic never dies. Finish your espresso, and we'll go."

The house on the Steps of the Virgin was old and tumbledown, the paint peeling off its walls, the shutters broken, the heavy oak door studded with rusted wrought iron, a house that was once fine and noble but had now fallen into near ruin. The door was flung open at once when I knocked, and the man there was beaming at me; suddenly the smile went and there was a look of dark suspicion there instead. He was a big man, in his early fifties, but his head only came up to my chin. He looked at me in surprise, very warily, and I said: "My name is Cabot Cain, and I came to see Signor Vito Giabianco."

The dark brows were heavy, the look was angry. "La Polizia?"

"*Non sono della polizia.* I come to him for help, and as a friend." I said again: "*Come un amico,* a friend."

He looked at Maria and back to me, and said roughly: "He is not here." The bells were ringing again, and it was something to do with noses; this man had a huge, bulbous nose, most un-Italian, and I remembered that the great pianist, when I had seen him...

I said: "Surely you must be one of the Giabianco family, Signore? I once had the honor of hearing the great Leonardo, and there seems to be...a slight resemblance? A family likeness?"

The dark frown was gone immediately. His whole face was transformed, a charming, delightful and delighted man. He spread his arms wide and laughed, and touched his nose and said: "*Eh, gia, quel benedetto naso!* A nose to remark upon, *n'e vero?* You are a pianist too?"

"No. Just a lover of good music."

"And the name, Signore, was...?"

"Cabot Cain. And this is Signorina Maria Christophorous, a friend from Athens."

He took her hand and bent over it, and held onto it a great deal longer than he need have, and Maria smiled at him, and all the latent enmity was gone. He stepped back at last and held the door wide, and said: "The house, like all of us; is not as good as in days past, but it is yours. Please come in, please, please."

He shepherded us into the narrow corridor, up a steep flight of stone steps, and into a fine old *salotta,* the marble half-columns around the walls stained and without their luster; the domed ceiling dark with the smoke of the years, the Travertine fireplace ornate and still splendid in spite of its discoloring. He bowed us into the room and said grandly: "Once my father's home, his great dignity is still on it. His piano, even."

It was a Steinway Concert Grand, a beautiful instrument, and he lifted the keyboard cover and touched the keys, and the sound of Mozart was there, and he said delightedly: "You see? Perfect pitch, absolutely perfect. This whole family, Signore, lives for music and nothing but music. Well..." He laughed. "A few other delicacies as well, but mostly music."

He turned then, almost casually, and hesitated just a trifle. There was a woman standing over by the window, a tall blonde girl of twenty-five or so, remarkably beautiful but looking a little out of place here. I couldn't at first think what was wrong, and then I realized that she was just overdressed; not garishly so, but enough to detract from the dignity, as our host had called it, of the old room.

He said, speaking quite carefully, almost hesitantly: "Signor Cain, Signora Christophorous, *permettetermi a presentare*...Signorina Lucia Vicchio. Miss Vicchio is also a pianist, and a very fine one indeed. Tonight she will play for my brother."

She came towards us, the blonde girl, her hand outstretched, smiling, a little forcedly I thought, but quite calm in spite of whatever was troubling her. She was a local girl, a Triestina, with long, long legs, and pale grey eyes, and long fair hair that was just let to drop down to her waist, quite loose and unarranged, but shining admirably; I wondered how many old-fashioned hours a day she spent brushing it. A hundred times after every meal they used to tell their children.

I took her hand and said: "If you give concerts, Signorina, I hope we may have the pleasure of hearing you one day."

She laughed; not the polite, sophisticated laugh I would have expected, but a laugh of genuine amusement. "Oh no, Signore Cain, I am an amateur. But perhaps...quite an accomplished one." Her Italian was heavily accented—the accent, light and lilting, of Trieste. She looked at Maria with a touch of wariness, took her hand, and murmured: *"Un piacere."*

An elderly servant came in, a bright old woman, with espresso coffee on a tray, and our host fussed over her, showing her just where to place the cups, and turned back to me: "I am, forgive me, Ugo Giabianco, and I imagine that you know my brother Vito has been away for a while, or you would surely not have come to this house. How did you learn he was returning tonight?"

Maria said quickly: "Jablanica. In Athens."

"Ah, then that's all right." The ormulu clock over the fireplace, a little slow, showed six twenty, and he looked at it and said: "He will soon be here. I wanted so much to meet him at...at the prison, but..." He shrugged. "Vito is a strange man. First, he must breathe the clean air of unconfined solitude, alone, and so he will walk for a while, and when he is sure he is ready, he will come home."

There was a sadness there, but Ugo smiled quickly and said: "We do not try to hide the fact that he has been in prison for a long time, so trivial a crime. Vito never quite became good enough as a musician, none of us did. Some of us struggled to earn a living in, let us be honest, in mediocrity, but not Vito. Vito always wanted everything of the very best. The best houses, the best wines, the best food, the best women..." Almost subconsciously he glanced at Lucia; and I knew then what it was that had seemed out of place.

And so did Maria. She looked at me quickly, and then away again, and there was that imperceptible smile at the corners of her mouth; as though she found something very satisfying...

Lucia was standing at the window, looking down on the street absently, and she turned now and said, a statement, not a question: "*E lui*, it's him."

Ugo Giabianco froze, a coffee cup in one hand ready to pass to me, his eyes wide, his mouth half open, his head cocked to one side. He said: "Ssshhh," though nobody was speaking. He went quickly to the door and opened it a trifle, and then we heard the door being opened downstairs.

Almost surreptitiously, Ugo closed his door gently, and stood back and waited, and I felt now that our intrusion was acute. We heard the slow steps on the stone stairway, and a shuffling just outside, and then the door opened again and Vito Giabianco was there; and as Lucia had deduced, it could have been no one else but a man just out of prison.

His frame was gaunt, and wrapped in a heavy old overcoat, though the evening was warm. He was tall and awkward, and he had the huge family nose, and sparse grey hair and hard, hard eyes. His mouth was thin and bitter and unsmiling, and he looked about ninety years old. He stood there in the open doorway for a moment, his eyes on the piano; it was a long, long moment, and he was savoring something that had almost been forgotten. And then, with a gesture, he shrugged off the overcoat and let it fall to the floor, shrugged off the past with it too, and then he strode forward as his brother came to meet him, his arms outstretched.

They held each other tight, and kissed each other on the cheeks, and neither of them said a word.

The old man seemed to grow in stature in those seconds, as though he were only now aware of his freedom, that he was no longer an animal confined behind bars, behind the dark overdoor that shut out the light and the sights and scents and sounds of the beautiful Mediterranean world. His shoulders seemed to broaden, and he clasped his brother tight to his shoulders and shook him silently, and Ugo was crying unashamedly, the tears rolling down the red, bulbous nose.

It was quite a moment. And then the mood was broken as the door to the other room opened and the elderly maid came stumbling in, reaching out to embrace Vito too, weeping her old heart out. Ugo broke away and began to scold her, wiping the tears from his face with the back of his hand, but all he could say was: *"Basta, Mama, basta, basta..."*

The old lady took Vito's hand, kissed it, reached up to touch his face, and then turned and fled back to the kitchen to weep and enjoy the pleasure of her tears, the pleasure of the master home again after all these years.

Vito took a long deep breath and looked around the room. His eyes lingered on Lucia, and the blonde girl stood there waiting, smiling slightly, surprisingly poised and regal. He looked at Maria and did not smile, and then at me, and Ugo said hurriedly: "They came to wish you well, Vito. Signor Cabot Cain, Signorina Maria Christophorous...my brother Vito Giabianco."

The old man shook hands gravely, but his eyes were suspicious. He used his left hand; there was a heavy grey bandage around his right. And then he looked across at Lucia, and there was a delicate little moment when it seemed to me that he was quite aware of why she had not been introduced at the same time we were; he caught the nuance in the omission, and his eyes dropped, almost instinctively, to her breast—a fine Triestina breast, firm and pointed and full—then back to her pale grey eyes.

Ugo said: "And this is Lucia Vicchio, Vito, a fine, fine pianist. She will play for you tonight."

The old man nodded. "Good." He moved over and took her hand, and held onto it, and said softly: "And what else do you do, Signorina?"

Her eyes were on his, and there was quite a charming smile on her lips, as though she were delighted that he had found out the secret so quickly. She said, with just a little shrug of the shoulders: "What else do I do? I make love."

Ugo said softly: "For you, Vito." Only then did he look across at Maria; as though challenging her to find something offensive there.

The old man said again: "Good." He looked her up and down, then turned slowly to me and said politely: "It was good of you to come, Signore. May I ask who sent you to me?"

I said: "Your nephew, Jablanica. It seems that you were prepared to offer some information to a friend of mine, a man named Matthias Fenrek. About some bank robberies?"

Ugo said, quite shocked: "Then you *are* from the police!" There was an immediate hardening of the atmosphere.

I said quickly: "Not exactly. Fenrek is a friend, and he's in trouble. He's been kidnapped. I want to find him."

Ugo began to protest again, but Vito held up a hand for silence and said: "No. I know what this is about."

I looked at Lucia and said: "I'd have chosen a more propitious time, but..."

"Yes, I understand your urgency. A man who is kidnapped is very often killed, is that what you want to say?"

"That is what I want not to say."

"And there is something that you must understand, too. Is it reasonable for you to wait, while an old man satisfies his animal lusts on the body of a beautiful young Triestina girl? No, of course it is not. And yet, that is what you will do. You must understand my urgency. For five years. Oh, five years is not a long time except for an old man, but that is what I am, and my years are valuable to me now. And almost all of them, in solitary confinement. Can you understand what that is? One hour a day for exercise if the guards remember, or bother. The rest of the time, caged in silence, nothing to do but think...Yes, you will wait until I am ready for you." He saw that his brother was shocked, and he smiled quickly, a sour, cynical smile, and said: "A tight little family, Signor Cain, and you are an outsider. That shocks my brother, to hear me be so rude to a guest. But I know that you understand. I know that you are a man to whom I can speak frankly. Am I right?"

I said: "You are right, Signor Giabianco. If you would rather we came back. Tomorrow, perhaps?"

"No. Bear with me for a little while. There is a lot I have to tell you, but first... First, I must get the stench of that *benedetto carcere* out of my nostrils. With music, with love..."

He broke off, and held my look, and said: "For a few minutes, to forget all that."

He held out his bandaged hand to me and said: "You see this? Every bone in it shattered. Less than a week ago, when they told me the day and time of my release. For more than four years of the five I served, I had been in solitary confinement, not a very good prisoner, you understand? I beat up a guard sometimes, I stole rations, I was offensive to the authorities, a crime they can never stomach." He laughed shortly. "And so, most of the time I was in solitary. But when the news of my release came through, they put me in the yard with the other prisoners, and there..." He sighed. "You must know about Cernik? Klaus Cernik?"

I looked at him and said nothing. It didn't seem wise to say that I'd never heard the name.

He went on: "Cernik did this to me. Three of his friends held me down on the floor, and Cernik stomped on my hand until it was a mass of blood and shattered bones, so that I would never again play the piano, you understand? A warning of what would happen to me if I told...Fenrek, or anyone else, the things I know. He would have killed me, but if he had done that—well, it is easy to talk your way out of minor trouble, trouble of this sort. But a killing, no, he would never have gotten away with it. And so, he just taught me a lesson, a lesson in *omerta*, in silence."

"And you accepted that?"

"No." His voice was firm and hard. "Not for this. The protection of *omerta* is for the legitimate criminal, for a man like myself. It does not protect a man like Cernik." He turned to his brother and said sharply: "Is there no wine in the house?"

It was strange how Vito's acceptance of my presence brushed off on Ugo, and I thought for a moment of the tightness of this very Italian family, with Vito the undisputed head, a man whose wishes, whose thoughts even, were quite binding.

Ugo nodded and found glasses and a bottle of Chianti, and Vito turned to Lucia and held out both his hands to her, beckoning with the tips of his fingers, curling his hand at her as an uncle might to a young niece. She came over to him slowly, and he touched her lightly on the arm, and said: "Will you play for me now? Chopin, perhaps? It is so long since...so long."

She reached out and touched the grey leather of his face, and her voice was very soft and sweet: "Yes. I will play for you now. I will bring back some memories."

It was as though Klaus Cernik had been quite forgotten. Vito sank down into an easy chair and rested his head back and closed his eyes, and Lucia sat at the Steinway and began to play. Maria and I sipped our Chianti and listened, and Ugo stood at the window with his eyes closed and listened too, and then the old servant came and stood in the doorway in silence, a silence that was unbroken by any of us as the major-minor vacillations of the Nocturne in B fell delicately on the air.

Nobody spoke, nobody moved. Lucia's talent was tremendous, and she embellished the coruscating coloratura with an authority that was remarkable. And why not? Should a woman not be a great pianist merely because she is also a prostitute? And when it was all over, the old man sighed, and got to his feet, and went over to where Lucia sat waiting for his approbation, and he took her by the hand without a word and led her gently into the bedroom.

For a long time we sat there in silence. It seemed as though the notes of the piano were still floating on the air. It might have been a time for awkwardness, but it seemed to me to be perfectly natural that we should sit there and wait while in the other room a sad old man was trying to recover his dignity with the help of a young and beautiful woman; and so, we said nothing, and we waited.

And then, at last, there was a sound from in there, a frightening, unexpected sound, the sound of a high-pitched scream that seemed as though it would never end. Ugo ran to the door, but I was there ahead of him, my shoulder against it, always the quickest way to get a door open if you carry two hundred pounds around with you.

I was thinking of Cernik and the warning, and *omerta*. But I was wasting my thoughts. The door smashed to the ground, and Lucia was there on the bed, naked and lovely, staring down at the face beside her, a white face in which the open eyes were looking up at the ceiling quite sightlessly. Her hands were at her face, and the scream went on and on and on until at last she caught her breath and sobbed, and turned to stare at me and said, a single, terrified phrase: "*E morto*. He's dead."

It was his heart, of course, but I had to be sure. I saw that the window was wide open, the cool air streaming in from the distant sea. Lucia was sobbing bitterly, and I put a hand under her chin and lifted it up and asked: "He died like that?"

She nodded. "Like that."

She wrapped the white sheet around her body, a shroud, and went back to her sobbing. Ugo stood there looking at his dead brother, and he turned to Lucia and said, his voice very low: "Did he love you? Did he take you?"

She stopped crying and tried to dry her eyes on the sheet. "Yes. He took me."

Ugo took a long, deep breath, and pulled the sheet across the naked thighs, and sat on the edge of the bed and put his hands to his head.

Maria and I stole out of there, in silence, feeling the guilty weight of oppression, as though we had been spectators uninvited at a domestic tragedy that was, after all, no concern of ours whatsoever.

And after the cool silence of the old house, the noisy, dusty bustle of the hot street was at once a relief and an agony.

CHAPTER 3

We tied up the Monterosso phone in my room for more than an hour when we called B7 in Paris.

I have no official standing with Interpol; indeed, if they knew to what extent I'd insinuated myself into Fenrek's affairs, he'd probably be drummed out of the Service, so we always keep it a deathly secret. It was therefore Maria who had to start the ball rolling.

First, she identified herself by number and code name, and then waited while the voiceprint machine ran a check on the tape and confirmed the identification. (Once I'd called the night duty officer in an emergency and told him that I was Fenrek, knowing that the duty officer was a new man and couldn't possibly recognize Fenrek's voice. But the print check went to work and a policeman was knocking on my door before I'd even finished the call...) Once all that was established, Maria tried to track down someone who knew me personally, well enough to give me a few trade secrets. She repeated the code names I gave her, one after the other: "Claudius? Tacitus? Lucius, perhaps?"

No, they were all out of town. But finally, we settled on a man known as Passienus, an old friend I hadn't seen in a long time. He was spending the night in Fenrek's own apartment on the Boulevard Souchet that runs from Auteuil to Passy, along the edge of the lovely Bois de Boulogne, which was handy, because Fenrek's place, of course, is fitted out with the necessary telephone security.

I waited patiently for the *ping-ping-ping* sound that meant the line had been checked for any possible taps, and said cheerfully:

"Passienus? How's Agrippina?"

"Ha! Well I'll be damned!"

It was an old joke among just a few of us, and it meant that he knew at once who was on the line. Some years ago, when he'd first been given the code name Passienus, his rather dowdy wife—he had married her, he told everyone, merely because she was such an excellent cook—had fed him some special mushrooms she'd picked herself in the Bois; special indeed; among them was an *Amanita phalloides*, one of the nastiest and most deadly poisonous plants in the vegetable world. She sat by his hospital bed in tears for days, and the first thing he'd said to her on his recovery was the single word: "*Agrippina!*" Agrippina, of course, not only poisoned the Emperor Claudius, but also her own husband, Passienus.

I said: "You know who it is?"

"Of course."

"Well, how is she?"

He said promptly: "She's fast asleep in the other bedroom, and that's where and how I like her best. What are you doing in Trieste? Is our friend with you? If so, I have to speak with him, he's been out of contact and something's cropped up. Is he there? And how've you been keeping? It's been a long time."

I said nothing till he dried up. I looked at Maria and said: "He always had your problem, he talks too much."

I could almost hear the silence at the other end, and then there was a short laugh. "All right, put our friend on the wire."

"He's not here, that's what I'm calling about."

"Well, in that case, when you see him..." He broke off abruptly, and said: "My God, can you hear that?"

"I can hear it."

There was a faint, undulating whistle on the line, almost like a static interference; it meant that the tap check had switched over to positive; that meant, in turn, that someone had just opened up a tap on the line, an almost unheard of occurrence with an Interpol phone.

He said, his voice sounding a bit forced: "I'll have to find that out, so I'll call you back in ten minutes or so."

Ten minutes; just nice time to go out and find another phone. I said: "You're out of your mind."

Passienus was once Fenrek's man in Nairobi, and his Swahili, in those days, was near perfect, so I simply switched languages and said: "The chances of anyone understanding us now are infinitesimal."

"Oh. Yes, I suppose you're right." It was still fluent.

I said: "Well, the old man's disappeared, and the chances are that he's been kidnapped. His associate here was investigating some bank robberies, which has got to be a lot of balls. I want to know what he was really up to."

He began pedantically: *"Neno alilolisoma ambalo hatutalisahua,* one thing he said which we must not forget, is—my cover must not be broken, under any circumstances whatsoever."

"Good. Then he has a cover story. What's underneath it?"

Passienus said: "My God, don't you understand what I just told you? *Under no circumstances whatsoever,* he said. He'd have my guts for garters if I told you that."

I said patiently: "If he really has been kidnapped, he'll string you up if you don't tell me, and you know it."

There was a long silence at the other end. Then: "All right. There's a name, how do I spell it out for you?"

"Put it into LMT code, based on—remember the name of the bistro we used to drink *pastis* at?"

"I remember it."

"Use the name for the code."

"Right. Hold on."

I waited while he worked it out, and I said to Maria: "Write down the letters: P-a-i-l-l-a-r-d. LMT code." The Paillard, on the corner of Chaussee d'Antin and Boulevard des Italiens, was once our favorite rendezvous; they have the best *pastis* in Paris.

He said at last: "R-s-s-x-p-u-a. Got it?"

"I've got it." Maria was scribbling furiously, working out the code.

Passienus went on: "This man is a Greek terrorist, from way back, from nineteen forty-one to be precise. Does that mean anything to you?"

"Go on."

"He was executed by the British on Christmas Day that year, but did you know?" He said piously, "you should never shoot anyone on the Lord's own day, they always come to life again."

"Meaning?"

"Meaning that it seems now they shot the wrong man. That same terrorist has just turned up again, nearly thirty years older and a lot more deadly."

"How old was he when he was shot?"

"Eighteen. Sad, isn't it?"

"And now?"

The shrug at the other end seemed to come humping its long way down the wires to me. He said: "*Kwari* the hell *kuniuliza?* Why ask me? You know our friend. Everything he does, he does on his own."

"One question. Does the Political Section know what he's up to?"

A long pause. Then: "Why do you ask?"

"Why don't you answer?"

He sighed. "Well, I thought it was strange at the time. He stopped the routine memos that in the normal course of events would have gone to Political. Said we needn't bother them with this. A bit irregular, I thought. You know what it means?"

"Yes."

He sighed again when I didn't sound like explaining. I asked him: "Anything you can tell me that might help me to find out where he is?"

"Who, the terrorist?"

I said patiently: "First, we'll find the boss. A question of priorities, wouldn't you say?"

He sounded hurt. "Absolutely nothing, I'm afraid."

"Then tell me what the link is to the terrorist?"

I could detect the signs of nervousness back there in Paris; he didn't like talking quite so openly about his superiors affairs, even in an emergency. He said hesitantly: "All I can tell you, really, is that a report came in from Greece of a particularly brutal killing in Florina, just over the border from Yugoslavia."

"I know where Florina is. Who was killed?"

He said: "Here we go again with that damned code. Couldn't you just come to Paris instead?"

"Same code, work it out, it exercises your mind."

Maria had finished, and was holding up the paper for me to see. The decoded word turned out to be "Agathon." I gave her the fresh batch of letters as he dictated them to me, and he said:

"This unfortunate fellow was very brutally murdered, together with his wife and sister, and a bright young cop succeeded in extracting a single fingerprint from a bloodied tile. It belongs to that terrorist, and therefore, he's still alive."

"No doubt of that, I suppose?" They are pretty thorough in the fingerprint section at Interpol, but a smudged print...

He said didactically: "No doubt at all. One of the villagers saw the three men getting the hell out of there, and even the description fits with what he would look like now."

"And what else have you got on him?"

"Nothing."

"And that was enough to send Fenrek scuttling to Greece? I don't believe it."

I could sense the shrug. "That's all there is."

I said: "The year nineteen forty-one—we're talking about a certain terrorist organization in Greece, are we not? The big one?"

"We are indeed."

"And the name you gave me sounds like a code name. Is it?"

"I assume so. They never used their real names."

"And that's a very strange name for a guerrilla leader to choose, wouldn't you say?"

He hesitated. "The original holder of that name was a Greek poet, I think, about the time of Plato, though I'm not too sure about that."

"Then you ought to be. He was born, your poet, in four forty-eight B.C., and died forty-eight years later at the Court of Archelaus, and yes, he was both a contemporary and a friend of Plato's."

Now the gentle undulation stopped; and the *ping-ping-ping* came back; it meant that the tap had been shut off, either automatically or by design, and that the line was now safe again.

Passienus said: "Thank God for that. Who the hell could be tapping the line, it's almost impossible."

"It can only be done from within the Department. And that

explains Fenrek's reluctance to keep Political informed, doesn't it? He must have suspected a leak somewhere."

"Yes, that makes sense. Why did you say that Agathon was a strange name for a guerrilla to choose as his *nom-de-guerre?*"

"Because your original Agathon was a flaming queer, that's what's strange. A fag, much derided for his effeminacy. And yet, our terrorist chooses it for his cover, it doesn't make any sense at all. The psychology is all wrong."

"Well, I don't think it matters a hell of a lot."

"Bad psychology always matters."

I have an M.S. in Psychology from Harvard, and if you study this much abused aspect of human behavior deeply enough, you can't help being inquisitive on such occasions. The terrorist group we were discussing was the old wartime ELAS, as tough a bunch of thugs as the world has ever seen. And here was one of them naming himself after a poet so gay that he wore women's clothes and went to bed with anything in pants, so effeminate and gentle that he wouldn't even step on an ant. It made no sense at all.

I said: "Get me a rundown from Special Index on a man named Klaus Cernik. He's in prison in Trieste just now. Hold on a moment."

He said quickly: "Are you in trouble?"

"No." It was just a waiter bringing the bottle of cognac I'd asked for. I'd had a feeling it was going to be a long session. When he'd gone, I said: "Okay. Klaus Cernik."

"I can put you through to Special Index, and they can give you all the info. Or do you want me to run over and get it for you?"

"Just put me through, tell them what I want."

"Do they have your V.P. on record? They won't say a word if they haven't, you know."

"If they've got my voice, I want to know why. But there's someone here who can take it all down. Put me through. And give my love to Agrippina."

"I will. Anything else?"

"Just keep quiet about our talk."

"Well, of course, I'm not an absolute idiot, you know."

"Really? How nice for you."

He sighed. "I'm switching you over to Special Index."

I gave Maria the phone, and said: "What was the name of the man who was so brutally murdered in Florina?"

She said: "Crespos. Stefan Crespos." Her paper was all covered with the crossword puzzle of the LMT Code. I poured cognac into two paper-thin tulip-shaped glasses with the Monterosso crest on them in gold, and when the security check had sounded again, she said: "Ready."

Her quick, nervous fingers were holding her silver pencil delicately, almost caressing it, as though it were a phallic emblem. She began to write rapidly, and I passed her a drink and saw that she was translating into Greek as she went along and then putting it into a mixture of Pitman and Gregg shorthand, together with a few abbreviations that seemed to be all her own. And when S.I. finally rang off, we had four pages, tightly and neatly spaced, about a man who a few hours before was only a cypher:

Cernik, Klaus, male Caucasian, born November 7, 1914, in Plovdiv, Bulgaria. Education: Grammar. School Plovdiv, Military Academy Sofia, transferred to St. Cyr, Paris; May, 1934...(A query in my mind there. St. Cyr accepts only French citizens. How had a Bulgarian come to attend a French Officers' School?)

...Transferred to Ecole Polytechnique, Paris, after eighteen months, graduated with Honors in all subjects, June, 1937...(Another query. St. Cyr trains for the Infantry and the Tanks, the Polytechnique specializes in Engineers and Artillery. He's getting both, very unusual treatment; why? And he finished each two-year course in eighteen months. Either a very bright boy, or...what?)

Greek Army 1939-1940 (What happened in the intervening two years), *discharged dishonorably with the rank of Colonel* (a Colonel at age 30? Common enough in America, unheard of in the European armies, particularly in Greece. What goes on?) *and disappeared, believed in Egypt. Captured while fighting with an ELAS group against the Greek Government in Kavalla, Greece, (Note: near Philippi) in December 1944* (Question again. Was he with Agathon then? The time checks out, and both of them were with ELAS.)

The schedule was carefully detailed, but there were great open gaps in it; for a few years, they'd know all about Cernik, and then another disappearance. He was with the American Army in West

Germany just after World War Two—an Intelligence Officer!—and was arrested there on charges of beating political prisoners, escaped, disappeared, was arrested in Turkey. Escaped again, turned up in Rio de Janeiro using the name Wilhelm Kittering, turned up again in Spain as Jose Mendoza and was under suspicion of forging checks, but disappeared before he could be arrested. On and on the record went, and at last they had him in prison in Trieste, accused of murder, held under maximum security.

Wrong again, I thought. *He's wandering around the yards with all the other prisoners, stomping on pianists' hands.*

There followed a detailed physical description in accordance with Interpol's highly efficient Bertillon System: height, reach, height seated, head measurements, length and breadth of the right ear, limb measurements, length of left forearm and left middle finger, and all the other intricate fol-de-rol that would identify Cernik at once quite independently of his fingerprints. A severed head can't be fingerprinted, but there's enough in the System Bertillon for positive identification.

His blood group was there, his fingerprint analysis, a note of his personal habits, and his ED figure, which was seven. ED represents the evaluation of the danger he represents under certain given conditions, and seven is very high. Vito Genovese, I remembered, at the time of his 1959 incarceration, was rated five, and Lucky Luciano never got past three.

So. Were we getting anywhere, or weren't we?

I fell into a sort of lethargic reverie, and Maria—what a lot of sense some women have!—just sat there in silence and filled my glass when it was empty. I looked across at her and studied those dark, intelligent eyes, and said at last, musing: "How's your Greek history?"

She was not surprised. "Adequate. Better than most people's, I suppose."

"Tell me about a man named Agathon."

She said promptly: "A playwright, more than a poet. He's credited with inventing the plot as an essential part of a story. Before his time, a play was just a matter of vaguely connecting details, cause and effect, victories and their aftermath. Agathon put them all into perspective and made them into a plot. He was also the first man to use a choral ode which was not part of his story. And, as you said, he was effeminate, weak, gullible, and the laughingstock of the Athenian Court."

I put my feet up, let the warmth of the cognac suffuse my palate, and tried to put myself inside someone else's mind. I said:

"Three groups, fighting a Civil War in Greece, one of the most vicious little wars in history. There was ELAS, there was EAM, and there was EDES; and the most violent of these was ELAS, which called itself the National Popular Liberation Army. They fought the Germans first, and then their fellow Greeks, and they were finally put down with British troops and American money—the Truman Doctrine of March twelve nineteen forty seven. But those years...Brother against brother makes for the worst possible kind of war, doesn't it?"

She didn't answer; she was Greek, and it was a personal thing for her. Greece's greatness stems, in part at least, from the fact that it has gone through all these vicissitudes so often, over so many centuries of violent dissent.

I found it comforting that she could say nothing and still not detach herself from me; a silence between us was more intimate than talk. I found myself growing very fond of her, almost wishing she wasn't Fenrek's girl.

I said: "Agathon, the gay poet. Would you call him a famous man?"

She nodded. "Yes, I would." I was conscious that she was following my line of thought, trying to figure it out for herself.

I said: "Now go forward in history about eighteen hundred years."

"In Greek history?"

"Yes."

"All right. The wars with the Turks and the Venetians."

"More precisely, the year fourteen seventy-four."

She frowned. "The Battle of Skodra?"

"Uh-huh. Or Scutari, as it was then called. The Turks were moving up through Northern Greece, Albania, and Yugoslavia towards Venice, for a major assault. En route, they destroyed the city of Croia, the ruins of which are in Albania. But Albania was then called Schiperia, and its peoples were the descendants of the Epirots, who were really Greeks, though they pretended not to be, all mixed in with Venetians and recently immigrated Turkish tribes. After they destroyed Croia, they attacked Scutari..."

"The modern city of Skodra."

"Right. And they were thoroughly defeated there by the Venetians, largely because of a surprise attack on their rear by a small and highly mobile group of irregulars who swept down from the mountains during the night and cut them to pieces, then faded away before the Turks could gather their forces together for any kind of counter attack. They did this for four nights in a row, and so decimated the Turkish Army that they were forced to retreat, with their lines of communication cut to hell and gone."

The dark brows were drawn together as she listened. She said at last: "All right. The history lesson's over. What's the point of it?"

"The point is that those irregulars were led by a Greek General named Felas Agathon. And that's the man whose name our Agathon took. Nothing to do with the effeminate poet. An easy enough mistake; if you say Brutus, you automatically think of Marcus Decimus Brutus who stabbed Julius Caesar; but you could be meaning Brutus Gallaecus, or Brutus Albinus, or a dozen other Brutuses. Or should I say *Bruti?*"

She was *so* patient! "And Felas Agathon?"

I said: "Felas Agathon retired, an obscure and almost unknown soldier, to a little village in what is now Yugoslavia, less than eighty miles from his triumph at Scutari. He died there a few years later, unsung, un-mourned, a man who saved his country from extinction."

Her eyes were alight with excitement now. "And the village is called?"

I said: "When Felas Agathon died there, it was called Serpolis. Today, it's called Serigrad, and there's precious little there except ruins. But keep me on the right track. If you were planning to kidnap a man and hold him...for what? For how long? Is it at least a likelihood you'd try and do it in a place you knew well? So that he could be easily and securely hidden?"

"Yes, but," there was alarm on her expressive face now, "we don't know that they...that they didn't shoot him there and then, do we?"

"No, we don't. But I'll tell you again, Fenrek's not the kind of man to get himself killed quite so easily. If he'd believed he was heading for a quick bullet, he'd have made a run for it, even if it meant exposing you to danger. He's not the suicidal type."

I didn't tell her that there are people who walk into sudden death with their eyes closed, and people who do it with their eyes open, and that Fenrek belonged in neither of these two idiot groups; she'd never have bought so fragile an argument; she'd have said it was tenuous, and perhaps it was. But frankly, I just couldn't imagine that Fenrek was dead, and if you're going to start out with the assumption that your chase is futile, you're not really going to get very far. So, I said carefully:

"He wouldn't have walked into something like this unless he could turn it to his advantage. Believe me. I know him."

It took a little time for her to drive the fear away, and when it was gone, I said: "It all hinges on the fact that our Agathon chose that name. For what reason? Do you like coincidences?"

"No. I hate them."

"Good. So do I. So examine this one. Our terrorist took the name of Agathon, Felas Agathon, who lived and died at a known pinpoint within the area where we believe Fenrek to be a prisoner. Is it too wild a theory that he chose that name because he too came from the same place? I don't believe it is. And if our Agathon comes from Serigrad, isn't it likely that that's his base of operations? Or one of his bases? I could believe that."

She was excited now, but she wanted to be sure. "Make it a little clearer. A lot clearer."

"Our Agathon took his name from a boyhood memory, an obscure hero who lived and died in his own little village, its only claim to distinction. In other words, our Agathon's home town is the other Agathon's deathbed."

Now, she said it: "Tenuous."

It was a word Fenrek always used when he wasn't sure about my arguments, and I couldn't help smiling. Little bits and pieces of that man rub off on every woman he ever goes to bed with.

I argued: "Not tenuous. A likelihood. The coincidences are just too much for me to stomach otherwise. And don't forget a very important point; they must have known, once they found Fenrek alone, that you would have gotten in touch with the police. So they couldn't expect to go too far in that Citroen. Ergo, geographically, it works out just about right."

That clinched it.

The excitement had completely taken hold of her now. "So he's in Serigrad!"

I corrected her. "He *might* be in Serigrad. So that's where we're going."

I found a map and spread it out on the bed, and she gulped down her drink as though to make an end of it all, and leaned over the map with me, her perfume subtle and enticing. I pointed out the whereabouts of the little village for her, though it was too small to be marked on the map. I said: "You drove north from Gradsko for about an hour, bypassing Skopje, where you warned the police to be on the lookout, remember?"

"But there's no road."

"No marked road. But there's a dirt track here...and another here...that takes you right off the main highway and into the mountain tracks where a good car can manage quite easily, and they've got a Citroen, remember? It'll go anywhere, hydraulic suspension that can raise the body up by seven extra inches if they need it. The Delage would never have made it."

"Oh, my poor, beautiful car," she moaned.

"The Jensen can, because of its four-wheel drive, so we'll have no problems, so, let's assume they drove along this road here, and they came to Vrebestica, and turned off along the goat track that leads to Serigrad, once called Serpolis, an ancient ruin quite obliterated now by the forest, and five or six small wooden houses. Shouldn't be too hard to find him, should it?"

She jumped to her feet. "Do I have time to fix my face?"

The eagerness was touching. I said gently: "Don't count too much on it, Maria. Likelihoods nearly always pay off, but once in a while... We could be wrong."

"No." She said fiercely: "I know we're right!"

I smiled. "So go fix your face, you'll see him soon. But put on something sensible, we might be crawling around in the dark on our hands and knees."

She grabbed up her little case and almost ran into the bathroom. When she came back, she wore an expensive jump suit of wine colored, very fine wool, so delicately woven and fragile that it was almost invisible, something that nobody in her right senses would wear anywhere except on the cover of Vogue. It was open in the front almost to her waist, no buttons, no zipper, nor ties, nothing, just a silk scarf round her white throat.

I said again: "On our hands and knees in the woods."

She shrugged and said: "I've worn it before."

Ten minutes later, we were crossing the lazy frontier post at Bistja once again. The same border guards were still on duty there, and they smiled and looked at our passports briefly, and waved us on with a cheerful: "*Svoboda narodu*, freedom to the people."

Oh well, they've got to get the little bit of propaganda in there once in a while; doesn't hurt anybody, and it's nice to know that they care.

CHAPTER 4

The clock on the Jensen was chiming midnight.

It's a great advantage, a chiming clock in a car, and I'd only recently installed a custom-built Girard Perregaud, hand wound on an old-fashioned mainspring, its tiny bells tolling the hours and the quarters. I don't like taking my eyes off the road, even for a split second, when I'm driving over a hundred miles an hour in the dark.

The tall pines and hazels of the lovely Slovenian mountains met over the road, a dark green, tree-lined tunnel through which the powerful Lucas flamethrower lamps, a hundred thousand candlepower of Quartz Halogen in each of them, cast their long white beams for forty seconds of fast driving ahead.

The stereo was playing Katchaturian's "Spartacus", and the lively notes of the Phrygian Adagio thundered out of the four Lear Jet speakers. I could sense that Maria, huddled deep down in the soft hide of the bucket seat beside me, was nervous, and I said to her, patting a friendly knee: "Don't worry, I know how to handle a fast car."

A touch on the oscillating discs of the Maxaret braking system (you just can't skid with oscillating brakes, whatever the road surface may be) brought the speed down to sixty miles an hour as a felled tree swept past us, blocking half the road with its groping branches. It reached out for us briefly with its tentacles and forced us onto the wet and soggy verge. But the Jensen F.F. has four-wheel drive, with both axles locked in permanently, and I could feel the power of the front wheels hauling us back onto the road again the moment the obstruction was behind us. There's an exhilaration to driving a car of this quality, a sophisticated British chassis with America's biggest mill to drive it, a mixture that's impossible to beat; the soft purr of the engine was almost a lullaby as I touched the gas and we went up to a hundred and ten.

We by-passed Ljubljana by taking the side road, not much more than a track, that heads up to the high mountains where the headwaters of the River Krka bubble out of the rich soil, with driven snow above us now on both sides, then sped down to the River Kupa and crossed over the fine, tessellated stone bridge that's been there since the year 925, when Duke Tomislav, who later called himself *Rex Chroatorum*, King of the Croats, made his celebrated forced march from Rijeka (which the Italians still insist on calling Fiume) clear across the county to the Bulgarian border, taking time out en route to build bridges, cut through mountains, and establish hilltop fortresses to keep an eye on his very extended lines of communication.

The road was cobbled here, the sign of a small village ahead; we passed through it almost before I had time to slow down. On to Banya Luka at high speed once more, a detour across the farmlands once again to miss Sarajevo. We were already deep into Bosnia, and it was only three twenty in the morning. We'd covered two hundred and seventy miles exactly.

I said to Maria: "An average of eighty-one miles an hour, could your Delage have done that?"

She laughed. "Maybe. I know that I couldn't. Have you any idea where we are?"

"Just crossing briefly into Herzegovina, back into Bosnia thirty miles up the road, and we're almost there. Hungry?"

"No. I could do with a drink though."

"Cognac in the glove compartment."

"Ah, good." She found the silver flask and sipped from it, then passed it to me and said: "Remy Martin, Fine Champagne, you're a highly civilized man, Cabot Cain."

"Yes. And not many of us left."

Djelasnica dropped behind us in silence; at this hour of the morning even the dogs were asleep, and I found the track I was looking for just past the heavy wooden beams that were a farmers' bridge over the rushing Zeljezia Bistrica, not much more than a deep stream here, the waters, snow fed, coursing over the grey granite boulders down there in the gorge more than a hundred feet below us. There were no side rails to the bridge, and we were safely over at speed before Maria had time to finish her anguished squeal. I swung the wheel hard over, the car bounced crazily over a shallow ditch where the mud was black and sticky, and into a plowed field, then swung it back hard again for the short cut to where—if things hadn't changed too much in this unchanging world since I was last here—the old granite-block road ought to be that Ivo the Black had built with slave labor in the late fourteen hundreds.

Well, it was still there, grown over heavily with long grasses and thyme and wild basil; the smell of the herbs was ripe and sweet on the night air as the wheels crushed them. A mile and a half and the road was gravel again, much wider, deeply rutted by the iron wheels of heavily laden carts that brought hazel saplings down from the mountain every spring.

The gas gauge warning light was glowing faintly in the darkness, a silent, pale-blue gleam, and I leaned down and switched on the reserve tank; another twelve gallons, or a hundred and seventy miles, before the Jensen needed a fill up. The gravel road came to an abrupt end and was a field once more, and now I had to slow down for the last climb to the top of the hill.

Above us, high up on the mountain, the old stone ruins of a fortress stood out sharply against the sky. I found myself thinking of the days when the great *Viadika* Peter the Second, the soldier-statesman-Bishop, first brought his rough code of law to these wild mountains; was it really only a hundred and forty years ago? The rest of Europe, by that time, was more or less civilized under law, but in these broken mountains, banditry was still, then, the common way of life, and it was not until Peter's time that a man could safely ride through them without a rifle at his side and a sword on his belt.

I dropped down to second gear, and we went up the incline fast, our nose pointing almost to heaven, bouncing crazily over a grass-covered field.

Maria said, alarmed: "Oh, no!" She was almost lying on her back, and she pointed out of the window and said: "For God's sakes, there's a road of sorts over there."

I nodded in the darkness. "A gravel road. It'll show our tracks. Here the grass will spring back to normal in five minutes. Get ready for some walking."

"Oh?"

I pointed: "There, on the skyline. Serpolis, that Felas Agathon knew as Serigrad."

She stared. "I don't see it."

"Just five houses left now, but it still calls itself a village. Hold tight."

I swung the wheel round again and drove hard into a clump of bushes. The rustle as they closed about us spelled trouble for the Jensen's bodywork; but it also meant security. I backed up a trifle, eased her to one side, and rammed in hard, crashing through the bushes and ruining the expensive paint job entirely. I said to Maria: "Stay comfortable for five minutes while I finish it off."

It would have been impossible to open the door, but the top was down, of course; I never see any point in putting it up except in cases of dire emergency, and this wasn't one of them. So I vaulted out over the side, squeezed through, took the long hunting knife from under the seat, cut a dozen branches, and in no time at all had the Jensen sealed off from the rest of the world, so that even the morning sun, coming up in fifty-two minutes now, would never find so much as a gleam of polished paint to give away our position.

I helped Maria out and whispered: "We have less than an hour, we'll have to move fast."

She was not impatient; confused is more the word. She whispered back: "Where to, for God's sake?"

I pointed. "We've got to keep that pump under observation, and wait."

"Oh."

None of the houses in this part of the world has piped-in water. They share a common well, or a pump, strategically placed, and every morning the women go down and fill up their pots and pans and basins, a social moment of early morning gossip.

A single tall column of stone blocks was on the skyline, standing straight and stiff and useless, all that was left of the old

Serpolis except for some hidden stones now covered over with trailing vines and dense undergrowth. The upper-most stone of the pillar, I remembered, was carved with the words: *"Will they remember me after I am dead?"* The sad thought of a great leader who had been forgotten in his lifetime. No, they had not remembered; when you heard the name Agathon these days, it meant a driveling fag, and nobody else. Should poetry, even bad poetry, last longer than the epics of soldiers? I suppose it should.

Somewhere below the stones, and close by in a little hollow in the dark hills, was the tiny village.

We climbed slowly, carefully, to a small bluff that, by my reckoning, ought to give us a commanding view of the backs of the five houses and of the wrought-iron water pump as well. The bluff was thickly wooded with old pine and young hazel, the forest floor soft and scented and friendly, and we found a spot where we could lie down together under the cover of protruding boulders, the lichen draped heavily around them, and were as well hidden as the car was half a mile below us. The village was invisible still, darkly shadowed. Soon, the sun behind us, it would be brightly lit.

The silence was acute, the air fresh and cold and damp. I heard a slight sound close by, and laid a hand on Maria's wrist for silence, but it was only a covey of birds moving through the fallen leaves, walking the ground close beside us.

I listened to them for a while, and then clicked my tongue quietly; they took off with that peculiar, anguished flutter, and I whispered: "Grouse, that's good."

It was too dark to see her frown. She whispered: "What's good about it?"

"The grouse's principle food is the wild bilberry."

She sighed, very patiently, and I whispered: "The blue on the dead man's lips, remember?"

"Oh."

The wild bilberry, sometimes called the blaeberry or whartleberry, or the *Vacciniim myrtillus*, if you prefer, is much tastier than its cousin the blueberry; it is also much more persuasive as a stain, and if you eat more than a handful of them your lips are going to be a bright, bright blue for a long time to come, it's quite indelible.

I said: "Your dead man, he'd been eating bilberries, it's nice to know they're growing around here."

She said again: "Oh." The white at her throat was gleaming in the darkness, soft, lucid, tantalizing.

I was wondering exactly how to get into the house, once we had located the right one. I wished we could go in under cover of the darkness, but the question of identification was important; it wouldn't do to go bashing into each one in turn, hoping we'd turn up a captive and contrite Fenrek. I thought I might just have to throw Maria at them, as bait, and I wondered if she'd mind very much.

The sun came up, a pale, pale yellow over the hill behind us, and in the first few moments of a grey wispy dawn, the little cluster of frame houses was lonely, and quiet, and impossibly peaceful. We could see them quite clearly now. No stores, no church, nothing but five frame houses perched at odd angles above the little hollow where the water pump was, their fences covered with trailing creepers, with apple trees gilded with the early rays at the very tops. A rich blue smoke was beginning to pour from one of the chimneys, then from the others; the villagers were stirring.

Soon, an elderly women came out from one of the houses and walked down to the well with a huge aluminum pot on her hip. She wore a black peasant dress, and I took the glasses from Maria and saw that she had quite a creditable moustache, a tough, leathery face and alert, intelligent eyes.

I watched her while she swung the iron handle of the pump vigorously, watched the white water pouring out. And then two other women joined her. She stopped and sat down on a tree stump to gossip with them. The other two were younger, plumper, moved more quickly; they both carried terracotta pots. One of them was quite pretty, a robust, strapping young woman of twenty-two or so, with long, straw colored hair that fell to her waist, and a simple, old-fashioned skirt and blouse, patched here and there with odd pieces of cloth. The other was just a child, perhaps fifteen years old, still heavy with puppy fat, a round, freckled face and jet-black hair that was cut short. The very fair, and the very dark; the races were all intermingled here, Croat and Serb, and Greek and Turk, the descendants of history's warring tribes.

I couldn't take my eyes off the fair woman; she held her head under the tap and laughed as the young child pumped vigorously at the handle and sent a stream of ice cold water playing over it; even up here, we could hear her delighted scream, and then, laughing, she swung her hair back and forth, weaving her head from side to side, bent over so that it almost touched the ground.

Maria whispered: "Look at that hair."

I said: "Ssshhh."

Now a fourth came out to join them, a middle-aged housewife with her dun-colored hair carelessly wrapped up on the top of her head and kept there with pins, and I whispered to Maria:

"The house under the plane tree, the only one that's not fetching water. And it's the only one that seems to have bilberries growing around it, though we can't be too sure about the others, can we? Not until we take a closer look."

The four women were chatting and laughing, and their voices came up to us, incredibly clear on the still, crisp air of the morning. One was washing out clothes, letting the water overflow from the trough and puddle the ground.

I held the glasses on the house under the plane tree. The ground floor windows were shuttered, but as I watched someone threw open the jalousies, leaning out to fasten them open with little wrought-iron clips that were cemented into the wall. It was a man, tousle haired, a white, collarless shirt, thirty years old or so, and squat-looking; his bare arm was like a leg of mutton, tremendously thick and muscular. But it was his thick dark eyebrows that interested me. I passed the glasses to Maria and said: "Quick, before he goes."

She snatched them and looked. Then he was gone, and she said: "Bulgarian? It's hard to tell. He could be Serbian, I suppose."

"Does he look to you like a local peasant?"

"No."

"Well, we still won't assume he's anything else. Not yet. We'll wait."

The women chatted on, and then a man came from the house—not the man we'd seen at the window, but a much younger one, not more than eighteen by the looks of him, a good-looking youth with a shock of very light hair, very unkempt. He was swinging a bucket and whistling to himself.

The women stopped their chattering as he approached. He was very polite. He stood aside, not speaking, until the woman who was washing her clothes made way for him. He bowed to her gravely, and said something I did not hear; she did not answer him; instead, she merely turned aside and waited for him to finish, and he nodded at the others and went off with his filled bucket. The women looked at him as he walked away.

It was a strange and inconsequential little drama, no more than a change of mood. The four women, so animated a moment before, were standing there, grouped silently together, four picturesque peasant women watching, with a touch of wariness, something that was alien to their tight little world.

The boy was a stranger, there was no doubt about it.

I swung the glasses round and looked at the houses carefully. There was only one that could be approached clandestinely. I whispered to Maria: "The house at the left, the one with the broken window."

"The good-looking girl, that's where she came from."

"I know. The only one we can get to without being seen. Down to the valley, skirt the wall close in, up under the apple trees, the fence will hide us all the way."

I gave her the glasses again, and she studied the layout for a while and said thoughtfully: "As we pass the wild strawberries there we can be seen from the upper windows."

"No, not if we go on our bellies."

"All right."

"Let's wait for them all to get home. I'll go in alone, you wait for me on the left of the outhouse, you'll see if anyone next door has spotted me."

"Sure you don't want me along?"

"Just keep your eyes open for me. If I need you, I'll let you know. Follow me."

The women were straggling back to their homes now, the two younger ones ahead of the others. I waited until they were inside, then carefully crawled from under cover and made a wide detour through the woods at our back. Maria was close behind me, moving quickly and silently from bush to bush with an efficiency that astonished me. I was reminded of the Partisan women, in the old days, who were even better than their men at this sort of thing, guerrillas who had fought in these hills from childhood. It takes very early training to move so stealthily.

We swung round as soon as we reached lower ground and the houses were out of sight, and ran fast to the little valley. Here was the danger, as Maria had pointed out; the wild strawberries covered the ground, tiny pinpoints of red on their long, trailing vines. I lay down on my back and eased myself along, keeping an eye on the upper window; it was barely within my sight, just the top, white-painted woodwork.

Now the fence was close at hand to hide us, and we walked quickly along it. I whispered: "Wait here, let me know if anything goes wrong. There, under the cart."

I watched her crawl on her hands and knees under the broken down four-wheeler, still piled high with long hazel saplings that soon would be burned into charcoal. I saw her grimace as she ripped the beautiful, quite impractical jump suit on a nail, tearing a long gash in it at her thigh. She lay down, hidden by a pile of barrel staves, and nodded at me, smiling, her eyes excited.

I went through the little white gate and up the garden path and knocked on the door, a gentle, not too insistent knock.

Close up, the woman was prettier than she had seemed through the binoculars, a fresh-looking country girl with dimples at the sides of her mouth, her hair braided now and hanging down over her shoulders, still wet, and she looked at me in considerable surprise. They're built to a very small scale, the houses here, and my head was above the lintel. Her pale eyes were wide, more amused than startled.

She said: "Well. And where did you spring from?"

A caller at this hour of the morning, a caller at any time of the day—an obvious foreigner in a neatly-pressed suit, which presupposed he wasn't hiking, and yet, no car visible... I saw all these thoughts tumbling over in her mind, and I smiled and said:

"I came from Titograd, on foot. I hope I'm not disturbing you? It's early for a social call, isn't it? But it's very important."

The smile was still there, and she corrected me gently: "Here we do not call it Titograd. We call it Podgorica."

Ha! The old Montenegrin name! We spoke Serbo-Croatian, but

she was pure Montenegro, and the old enmities die hard. There was a time when the two states were violent enemies, when the Montenegrins lived only for fighting. Even today, it's a standard joke throughout the whole of Yugoslavia that the Montenegrins have impoverished their land by constantly fighting for it.

She was looking behind me. To see if I were alone? To see if the neighbors were watching? Whatever it was, she seemed perfectly calm and relaxed.

I said: "Of course. From Podgorica. I wonder if I might talk to you for a while?"

"Oh? What about?" She was wondering whether to invite me in or not.

And that, in itself, was strange. In these parts, the rules of hospitality are very, very rigid. Any stranger knocking on the door—by all the old-fashioned rules, she was obliged to offer token food and drink. What was holding her back? I thought I knew.

I said: "I was looking for a friend of mine, a foreigner, who is supposed to be somewhere in this area. I thought perhaps you could help me."

There was suddenly a very wary look in her eyes, a look that was almost, but not quite, hostile; and I knew then that I was right. The foreigners in the house across the way meant, for her, something she did not like very much, and it showed; it showed that she wanted no part of them.

I said: "Please let me talk to you. My friend is in trouble, bad trouble, from another group of foreigners. I think they may be the ones in that house over there."

She stepped back quickly and said, very quietly: "Come inside. We've been expecting you."

Well, that was a surprise.

She closed the door behind us and led me into the plain square room that was living room, kitchen, and the main sleeping area. One corner was taken up by a huge square sugarloaf of a stove, a great tiled block in dun-colored ceramic, decorated with an old Serbian motif in yellow and brown, a narrow wooden plank bench running round its two exposed sides. On its top, the pile of cotton comforters was a foot thick, rumpled, not yet made up, and against the tiny black square that was its grill, an old enamel coffeepot was standing; there was the smell of fresh bread baking, and she said, very formally: "Sit down and be comfortable, you are a guest."

I sat on the bench and leaned back against the warm stove. She took a long wooden paddle and thrust it through the opening, brought out a loaf of warm bread, and found cheese and poured coffee, and when all the demands of courtesy had been taken care of, she looked at the comforters on the top of the stove and grimaced. "I haven't even made the bed up yet."

"It was very inconsiderate of me to call so early."

"Never mind. Eat and drink, and then we will talk. You are from the police, are you not?"

"No, not really. Why did you say you were expecting me?"

"I was expecting the police. We all were."

"Will you tell me why?"

She shrugged. "The men in the house there..." She broke off and thought for a while, and then smiled quickly and said: "It doesn't really make sense. They just don't *belong* here. They keep themselves hidden inside, they talk to no one, they speak Serbo-Croatian with a terrible accent, and...it just doesn't make sense that they should be there. Why would anyone come to this village to live? There is nothing here for tourists, they are not farmers, or woodsmen. Why should they come here?"

"And so?"

"So, we all thought that they were hiding from the police."

"Tell me how many of them."

"Six, I think. We were talking about them yesterday."

"We?"

"My father and I."

"Is he here now?"

"No. He went to Podgorica last night, to buy nails. He will come back this morning." The sweet-scented bread was warm and delicious, the cheese the pressed curds of goats' milk. She stood up suddenly and said: "Let me offer you grapes."

"You are very kind."

"It is not often a stranger passes." She said again: "You are not from the police?"

"No."

She found a jar in a cupboard, and scooped out six fat green grapes, heavily soaked in *slivovitza*, and handed them to me on a chipped saucer, putting it down on the wooden table, inviting me to join her. I moved over with my bread and cheese, and she brought the cup of coffee and somehow made an intimate business of it, and sat down across the table from me, cupping her chin in her hands and just looking at me. In these parts, it's not considered rude to stare. If you're a guest, and staying overnight, they watch you eat, they watch you wash, they watch you get undressed and under the comforters—it's all part of the idea of hospitality, which is in turn an essential part of their ancient philosophy. And if you give them trouble, they will draw a knife across your throat and watch you die, too.

She said at last: "What kind of trouble is your friend in?"

"I think he's been kidnapped." I said politely: "The bread is very good," and she nodded, very somber and serious all of a sudden.

"And you want to help him?"

"Of course. He is a friend."

"There are six men in the house there, and somehow...somehow they do not look like men it will be easy to fight against, not if you are alone."

It was a question, politely phrased, and I smiled and said: "I am not quite alone. My friend has a girl, and she is outside the house, watching it."

"You will need three or four strong men to help you. When my father comes—or there are two young men across the way. If you told them you need help... We are all quite sure that something is wrong there."

"When did they come here?"

She shrugged. "About six weeks ago. A big car, with six men in it."

"And the owner of the house?"

"A long time ago, it belonged to a family of Greeks who have always lived here. Or they might have been Turks. Their name was Kolettis, is that a Turkish name?"

"No. Greek." I liked the sound of it.

She went on: "The Kolettis family have lived here ever since I can remember, but there was just the old man and his wife, and they both died. A son came then. I don't know where he came from, but he did not stay long, and the house has been shuttered ever since, until about six weeks ago, when these men suddenly turned up and moved in." She shook her head vigorously. "They are not even Serbs, some other kind of foreigners." She smiled quickly, aware that she had made the term sound distasteful, and said: "You, too, I think, you are not really a Serb, are you?"

"No, American."

"American!" For her, it was a world she'd barely heard of. "But, but your family must be Montenegrin?" She was looking for a bond between us.

I used to teach the Balkan languages at the School of Advanced Linguistic Studies, and I was quite sure my accent had not given me away. It was my clothes. You can't look like a Serbian in a Brooks Brothers suit, it just isn't cut that way.

I said: "Is the car they came in still there?"

"Yes. In the stable at the back of the house. What will you do about your friend?"

"If he's there, I will bring him out."

"But you cannot do this alone."

"I must. I cannot drag your friends into a personal fight."

She was smiling now, frank and easy with me, quite composed and self-assured. She said: "Vrada and Kopec, the two boys I spoke of. If it's a question of fighting, they will not wait not to help you. They are true Montenegrins."

"No. These men are sure to be armed."

She shrugged, insisting: "The boys have their knives. One of them even has a gun, though I don't think it shoots any more. Something broke in it."

"How do I get into their stable without being seen?"

She said quickly: "If you cross over to where the lichgate is, and walk round what used to be the graveyard, there's a stand of hazel, quite thick. Go to the left of it, over the fence, and the stable is right beside you. There's no door at the back, but you can easily get through, some of the planks are missing."

I wondered how she knew so much so readily, and she read my

mind and laughed. "The old man, Kolettis, used to keep his apples there when I was very young, and we used to go and steal them from him."

"Tell me about Kolettis. The son, not the father. When did he come here?"

"It must have been about four years ago, I think."

"And he was then how old?"

"About forty, I suppose. It's hard to tell with the Greeks. His name is Otho, Otho Kolettis. I remember he was a very angry sort of man, he would speak to nobody, not even to say *dober dan*, good day. And his temper! One day, a dog barked at him, and he picked up a log of wood and smashed its head in, just like that. He would spend hours up on the hill there, just sitting by the ruins and staring out across the valley."

I interrupted her: "The ruins where the inscription is?"

She looked at me blankly: "The inscription?"

"The Greek lettering at the top of the ruins."

"Oh, that. Yes. I always wondered what it meant, that inscription."

"It says: 'Will they remember me after I am dead?' The words of a great fighting man who has been forgotten."

"That's very sad, isn't it? Nobody should be forgotten."

"And then?"

She said: "Will you smoke? I have my father's pipe if you would like if. There is tobacco."

"No, thank you very much. How long was the young Kolettis here?"

"A few months, I think. And then he went away, and the house was boarded up." She said urgently: "Let me get the boys for you, wait till my father returns, you cannot fight them alone."

It was time to go. I stood up and said: "You have been very kind. May I know your name? Mine is Cabot Cain."

"Cabot Cain. I am Anna Obrenovic."

There was suddenly an enormous dignity on her, another of the Montenegrin qualities. She was looking around the impoverished, barely-furnished room, and I said:

"There was a Serbian King Michael Obrenovic, who was

murdered in Belgrade on the night of June the tenth, eighteen sixty-eight."

She smiled: "My father is his great-grandson. Under the new regime, there is no room for Kings and Princesses any more, and we have become Montenegrins, peasants. The children of kings are killed, and their children are suspect, and the children's children. In the course of time, they become part of the people. And so, King Michael's great-great-granddaughter digs the soil, and draws water from the well, and grows bilberries for the market, just like anyone else." Again, that eloquent shrug. "And why should it disturb me? I have never known anything but hard work and poverty. It is enough."

I took her hand. "Good-bye, Anna. And thank you."

"Would you like cheese to take with you?"

"You are very thoughtful. Let me take a small amount to my friend's friend, outside."

"But why don't you bring her into the house? She can wait for you here."

"She has work to do. We both have work to do."

"And you won't let me call the boys?"

"No."

"All right."

She wrapped up some of the fine goat cheese in a sheet of paper torn from an old magazine and gave it to me. I took her warm hand again and left to find Maria.

CHAPTER 5

I waited a long time in the lee of the stable wall, lying there in the long grass and listening, wondering how Maria was enjoying the cheese.

All around me there was nothing but rubble, the kind of debris that always seems to collect outside a house that's been long abandoned: odds and ends of building stone, bits of timber, some rusting iron work, a trio of very old cart wheels, a bundle of staves and a half-completed barrel, all overgrown with long grass and the thorny bilberries which had so indelibly stained the lips of Maria's dead friend in the back of the Delage. I ate a few myself while I waited, enjoying the tart, pungent taste of them.

A pair of starlings in the eaves above me were chattering, quarreling noisily as I studied the lie of the land. On a caper of this sort, you go forward step by step, playing it off the cuff; and it's always well to absorb everything, every little detail that might be of value. A long iron bar lying in the grass—would I need a weapon? A line of gooseberry bushes running from the stable wall to the back of the house—would they give enough cover? A direct line down the hill to where Maria was in hiding—could I afford to run that way, in the open, trusting to luck?

The house itself, larger than most of the others, was a matter of a hundred and fifty feet from the stable, and the ground in between, once garden and orchard, was thick with tall weeds; a man could hide himself among them if he bent himself double and didn't waste too much time getting there. There were two windows overlooking the grounds on the lower floor, two on the second, and a third in the attic, up where the starlings were. I could see no signs that there was a cellar, but on the other side of the building the land sloped sharply away, and possibly...

I peered through the cracks in the timber wall and saw the car there, the same Citroen station wagon, its hood open. I didn't like that very much; you don't normally leave a motor exposed unless you're working on it.

I held my breath and waited.

Soon, a shadow moved in there, and then the polite young boy from the water pump moved into my range of vision, in overalls now, his hands greasy and black.

I waited again; no one else, just the boy working on the car. It was a question of speed now, and nothing else. Carefully, very gently, I hooked my fingers round a heavy timber beam that was lying among the weeds, and eased it clear of any obstructions. It was a hunk of six-by-ten-inch oak, a beam, no doubt, that was meant for repairs to the house, a heavy ten-foot length that must have weighed perhaps a hundred and twenty pounds.

I studied the wall of the stable, board and batten, one inch thick planks of redwood. I checked where the nails were, and where the inside studs must be, and I picked up the beam, balanced it just so in my arms, stepped back a couple of paces, and rammed it hard into the wall.

The board cracked noisily in two, shattered, and as I jumped through the gap it had made, shoving aside the adjacent boards, I wondered if the noise it had made would have been heard in the house; I thought perhaps not.

Then, I was on him.

He had swung round at the sound, his eyes wide, his mouth open, a heavy wrench already in his hand. He swung it up and back, a careless, wasteful movement, and I hit him once, quite gently, on the superficial cervical nerve on the side of the neck, using the point of my middle knuckle. He was out at once, cold as dead mutton; draped over the engine compartment of the Citroen, and I tossed him into a corner and waited to see if the sounds of my entry had caused any alarm.

Nothing. I took a good look around to see what there was to see.

It was just an old stable, now used as a garage, with some hay still scattered around, a few large barrels in one corner where the old Greek must have kept the apples that the Princess liked to steal. There were some old oil drums, a bale or two of dried-out straw, a dark leather horse collar, some reins draped over a nail, a much-decayed saddle, a few tools hanging on the wall, a big barrel of water, some long-dead onions hanging in strings, a few rabbit skins nailed out on boards, some bundles of old rags.

I found an adjustable wrench and undid the drain cock of the Citroen's gas tank, just enough for the gas to leak out in a nice, steady flow.

To my considerable surprise—he should have remained unconscious for a long time; perhaps I'd been too gentle—the young boy was beginning to moan audibly, so I thumped him once, a little harder, with the side of my hand over the posterior scapular, and he was silent again. I tossed him outside through the hole in the wall, soaked a rag in gasoline and took it with me when I climbed through after him. I felt it necessary to hide him from casual sight, so I piled some weeds over him, and then lit the rag with my Zippo, took cover myself, and tossed the burning rag inside.

There was the briefest of moments, and then, with a very demanding *whoosh!* the whole thing went up. In less than ten seconds the flames were licking at the wall I was lying against, the smoke billowing out in great dark clouds. I heard someone in the house shout, and I burrowed deeper into the rubble and waited. I heard men running, swearing loudly, yelling at each other, and when I judged that all, or most of them, were probably occupied with the fire, I got up and ran quickly along the line of gooseberry bushes, bent double and well out of sight, to the back of the house.

There's nothing really like a good fire to attract attention. Apart from the urgent need to do something about it, to stop the flames from spreading, it always seems to fascinate people; I wondered how many of them stayed in the house, if any at all.

I put my shoulder to the back door, broke it open, and ran quickly through the building, searching for whatever there was to find.

On the ground floor—nothing. Just a couple of rooms, one of them with a big tile stove in the corner, just as in the Princess's room, and with the remnants of a meal for half-a-dozen people. On a bare plank table: cheese, bread (stale), olives, and a bottle of *slivovitza*. The other room had once served as a more formal parlor, but it contained now only two mattresses on the floor, and a wooden table with a pile of old illustrated magazines, Bulgarian, on it.

I found a locked door on the other side of the house, a heavy timber door that had been fitted with a pair of very heavy padlocks, but since the door opened outwards they presented no problem; I simply put my foot against it and shoved, and at the third attempt the door came off its hinges. As I had suspected, it was a cellar. I ran down, broke off the boards that covered the small, high window, and took a good look around. There were a lot of very interesting things there.

First, there was a big crate that was labelled in Greek: POTTERY, DO NOT DROP. I found a crowbar and opened it up. It was packed tight with bundles of plastic explosive, wrapped in oiled paper, each hunk already with a detonator pushed into it and ready to be wired. I unwrapped one of the packets carefully, felt its texture and smelled it, and found it to be a fairly simple blasting gelatin, probably seven or eight percent of collodion nitrocellulose dissolved in nitroglycerin; simple, but formidable, with a detonation rate of some eight thousand meters per second.

Another crate marked: FRAGILE; HANDLE WITH CARE, contained a very unusual form of trinitrophenylmethyini-tramine, compressed info flat grey slabs about eight inches by four by two, each one of them powerful enough to create a great deal of havoc if anyone carelessly put a propellant anywhere near it. I found some picric acid, some ammonium picrate, and a small supply of what I suspected was cyclotrimethylenetrinitramine, and one thing was becoming increasingly clear; these people, whoever they were, were just plain bomb-happy. *None* of these things should be carried around in crates marked *fragile*. There was even a thick wad of an evil-looking substance that smelled like a mixture of potassium perchlorate, dinitrotoluene, and ammonium nitrate, which made it a chlorate explosive; and those things go up if you as much as sneeze in the wrong key.

Bomb-happy, there was no doubt about it; and with a casual carelessness that was terrifying.

I found eight Reising submachine guns, the Marine version of the old Thomson .45; thirty Garand rifles; a Simonov single-action, single-shot anti-tack rifle, the most crudely primitive piece of discarded plumbing the Russians ever turned out; a U.S. 2.36-inch anti-tank rocket launcher which got to be christened the bazooka in honor of the late Bob Burns' weird gas-pipe horn. And a large box of loosely packed pistols and revolvers, all carelessly jumbled up together: Walthers, Lugers, Berettas, American Colts and Japanese Nambus.

I could hear the flames over in the stable taking a good hold now. The men there were yelling at each other, telling each other where to slosh the water. I figured it would keep them busy for quite a while longer.

I went up the stairs again, and on up to the second floor. Two rooms here.

Very gently, I tried the door of the first room, opened it silently, and peeked inside. An unmade bed, two mattresses on the floor, a scattering of old magazines, four bottles—one of them full—three tin mugs, an unwashed dish that looked as though it had contained a tomato-based stew, and a very efficient short-wave radio. I closed the door silently, went to the other one, and listened.

There was only silence inside. I drew back my foot, thrust hard, and burst inside before the man at the window could turn round. He was busy watching the fire, and he swore and reached for the pistol that was on the small table by the window. I picked him up before he could get his hand on it and threw him hard at the wall, head first.

I didn't wait to see the damage he'd sustained; Fenrek was on the bed, his eyes closed, his face deathly white, not looking at all his usual dapper self. There was blood at the corner of his mouth, a terrible bruise under one eye, and a two-day stubble on his chin.

As I bent over him, he opened his eyes, stared at me, and whispered, his voice harsh and unrecognizable: "I didn't think you'd ever make it."

I said gently: "Any pain?"

He shook his head. "Just...woozy." He is Hungarian, and his English is immaculate, but a word like woozy just doesn't sit well on him, it comes out all wrong, all Eastern European. He said again: "Woozy, they've been...been using drugs."

I picked him up, and he said: "I can...can walk."

I said: "No, I'll carry you."

He was almost angry, a question of dignity, of an assertion of his own competence—which, under normal conditions, was very considerable. He swore, and said: "God dammit, I must walk on my own two feet, can't you understand that?"

Yes, I could understand it. I put him down and let him fall, and having made the point, picked him up once more and went with him out of the room and down the stairway.

Another man was moving up it, fast, running to get...what? It didn't matter. He stopped in shock as he saw us, one hand on the balustrade, a foot raised for the next step, his eyes wide and uncomprehending, six or seven steps below me. There wasn't time to do anything but kick out, so that's what I did, hard. My right foot caught him in the throat and he went spinning down the stairs to land with a fearful thump on the floor at the bottom. I clambered over his unconscious body, and ran back the way I had come, carrying Fenrek, light as a baby in my arms, frail and wasted and looking like hell, and ran with him through the apple orchard and over the fence to where Maria was waiting.

Fenrek was struggling now; trying to assert himself again, and this time I thought he could perhaps make it. I put him down gently, and Maria was all over him, kissing him and clutching at him, and behaving in general like a mother hen, and I said: "All right, cut it out, take him to the car, try not to be seen. Hurry."

She began to argue, and so did he, and I said: "Go on, get a move on, I'll keep watch for them, they'll be after us soon."

Maria took Fenrek's arm and they hobbled off together, keeping properly to the low ground, down into the valley well to the side of the pump, over to where the strawberry patch was and then in to safety among the trees and out of my sight, and anybody else's sight too.

The stable was a roaring furnace now; I could feel the heat of it even here. I kept low down behind the fence, out of sight, listening to the shouts and wondering just how long it would take them to realize that fires don't really start so easily, not when there's a mechanic around to take some sort of action before it gets out of hand. I wondered how long it would take them to find the unconscious youth stretched out among the tall weeds.

How many would there be now? Six, Anna had said. The young boy knocked out cold, the guard in the bedroom unconscious, one man half dead at the bottom of the stairs. Only three left, then.

I waited for them, and they didn't seem to be coming, so I left my cover and walked openly to where the fire was roaring away.

Right; there were three men who were the obvious strangers. A few villagers were standing by, watching and not helping at all, and among them I saw two husky youths grinning at each other, who looked just about right to be Vrada and Kopek, two tough, fair-skinned, blue-eyed, black-tousle-haired Montenegrins, their arms folded and their feet wide-spaced, bursting up out of the land that was theirs.

And then one of *them* saw me.

It was the man in the Citroen who had thrown the hand grenade that demolished Maria's Delage. He stared at me for a moment, and then yelled, and pulled a pistol out of his belt and got off two carelessly-aimed shots before I was on him. I broke his right arm quickly, so that he couldn't fire again, and picked him up and hurled him at the second man, coming at me fast now, a long dagger, Bulgarian by the looks of it, in his hand. He went down base over apex as his friend's body hurtled into him, and then the third man was running fast, running away and tugging at his belt. A good idea; he wanted to get out of reach before he started firing.

I was about to take off after him, but the two boys beat me to it. One of them yelled out: "Come on!" and leaped off in pursuit. The other—were they brothers?—followed, and by the time the man got his gun out and levelled, they fell on him together like hounds onto a wounded boar. They both hit him at once, and I couldn't help wincing as I heard the crunch that meant a very complicated breaking of the jawbone; not just a sharp crack but a very real *crunch*. I looked around at the villagers; two very old men, three women; a couple of kids. They all stared back at me solemnly, showing me by their silence that what I was doing was my business and not theirs. A little way away, the two boys looked at me and laughed, and one of them picked up the man with the gun and called out: "You want him, comrade?"

I waved back at them, and said: "Keep him, put him to work for you, make him dig the garden, draw water, carry firewood."

They both laughed delightedly, and one of them picked up the pistol and I turned away and walked over to the stand of hazel, cut round through the old graveyard and through the lich-gate—a fine old gate in heavy timbers; carved with the names of the Serbian patron Saints, and quite a remarkable piece of architecture; I took time out to look at the date carved across its lintel: *Stefan Cetinje Fecit, 1712 A.D.* That made it the time of Danilo the First, the first of the hereditary *vladikas*, or ruler-priests, who fought so bitterly against the Turks and the Greeks and the Bosnians and the Austrians, against anyone who wasn't a Montenegrin.

In a matter of moments, I was knocking on Anna Obrenovic's plank door again.

Her eyes were wider than ever, and she said, whispering as though we were conspiring: "Was he there, your friend?"

"Yes. He is safe now."

"Come in."

She shut the door quickly behind us, and stood leaning against it as though not quite sure of what was next, her hands behind her back, her eyes very alert and still amused, a bright and very charming young woman who might, except for the destiny of her country, have been a Princess.

She said: "Why did you come back?"

"I don't know. I suppose...I just wanted to thank you again."

"That wasn't necessary."

We could hear the crackling of the burning stable, and I said: "There's no danger. The trees are still wet from the night, there's just the stable to burn. It doesn't look as if the flares will reach the house. I wondered if I ought to compensate somebody."

It wasn't true. The thought hadn't occurred to me before, but it was good to talk to her. They'd need a little more time to get to the car, with Fenrek falling over himself, and Maria, in tears no doubt, trying to keep him moving. I went to the window and looked out across the green sunlit valley. There was no one in sight; they were keeping well under cover.

Anna said: "Vrada and Kopek were there, did you see them?"

"I saw them. As you say, they enjoy a fight. Good boys."

"And all the villagers have gone there too, it's quite a day for them."

"And you didn't?"

She blushed prettily: "I thought you might return. Do you have time for some wine with me?"

I looked at my watch. "Only a few minutes more, I'm afraid."

"A few minutes is all that...I'll get the wine."

She hurriedly opened the wooden cupboard and poured some red wine into white pottery mugs. "It isn't very good, I'm afraid." She held up the mug in a toast, and said gravely: "*Svoboda Narodu,* freedom to the people."

"*Svoboda Narodu.*"

She giggled suddenly: "It's always the *people* who have to be free, isn't it? Not each one of us, not you and I. Just...the people."

"You and I? They can never take our Freedom away from us unless we let them, can they?"

"No. No, I suppose not. But we Montenegrins—we've never been free, maybe that's best. If we were, people like my great-great-grandfather would conquer the world, and that wouldn't be right either, would it? Is the wine really terrible?"

I said gravely, telling her the truth: "It is excellent. Will you ask the two boys to do me a favor? Perhaps for the whole village?"

She said quickly: "Of course, anything, anything at all."

"There's a lot of explosives in that house, a lot of guns. If they could keep watch on the place, send someone down to Podgorica to bring a policeman—he'll know what to do."

She nodded: "I'll tell them." A little pause, and then: "Is there anything I can do? Not for the village. For you?" She held my look, her eyes very straightforward and honest.

I said: "Just...try not to forget me."

"How could I"

I stood there like an idiot, looking at her, liking her more and more all the time.

She said at last, very quietly: "And where will you go now?"

"To Trieste, perhaps. Or Skopje. I don't really know yet." I had to say something, to keep talking. "Have you ever been there?"

She laughed. "Trieste? Skopje? I've never been more than a few kilometers away from this house. I was born here, and one day I'll die here. In between...nothing."

"But you're happy?"

"Yes. I'm happy."

It was in her eyes, in her bearing, an attractive young woman who had nothing, and wanted no more than that. For a moment, I envied her. I wanted very much not to look at my watch, not to remind myself that by now Fenrek and Maria would have reached the car and would be waiting for me.

As though she were reading my thoughts again, she said solemnly: "Will you come back here one day, perhaps?"

"Perhaps. I would like to."

"There will always be cheese and bread to eat. You will always be welcome here."

I said: "You are a very gracious and lovely woman. I would like very much to come back, even for an hour or two, to talk with you. If I can, I would like to very much."

I took her hand and held it, a hand calloused with hard work but still warm and alive and promising. On an impulse, she stood on her toes and tried to reach, and I bent down and kissed her quickly on both cheeks; I wished that it were not so easy for people to get so fond of each other so casually.

She stood at the door and watched me go, and I ran quickly along the lee of the fence and over the strawberry patch and into the gully, and down through the forest; the last thing I saw as I entered the trees was her friendly figure, the long gold braids hanging down over her shoulders; she was waving to me, slowly and rather sadly.

They had found their way into the hidden car, and were sitting in the back seat like a pair of love-sick children, all close up tight as though nothing existed outside the confines of their own bodies. Maria had found the cognac again, and was literally pouring it down Fenrek's throat, and a flush was coming to his face.

I said: "Take it easy with that stuff, he's been pumped full of barbiturates."

"Oh my God."

Under the influence of the drink, his pallor had gone and his face was flushed, the eyelids drooping; his pulse, when I felt it, was far too fast, his breathing hoarse. He shook his head drowsily and muttered: "Don't *fuss* so much, I'm all right."

I took a good look at him now. The pupils were all wrong, the fever patches on his face mottled, his pulse racing and his extremities trembling. I said: "Injections?"

He nodded, and painfully rolled up the sleeve of his shirt to show me. The scars were raw, blue-tinged.

I said: "Diethylbarbituric acid, by the looks of it. In massive doses. You're *not* all right, and you won't be for some time to come. We'll have to get you to a doctor. Skopje's the best bet."

He shook his head, quite angrily, and said: "No! We have to go to Trieste." There was suddenly a look of shocked surprise, and he grinned and said: "My God, I got out of bed the wrong side this morning, didn't I? Is that what that damned stuff does to you?"

I said: "It makes a naturally bad-tempered man more so."

"My God, what a sonofabitch you are. But I thank you." He reached out and put a hand on my sleeve, and said: "They would have killed me in there."

"Lie back, make yourself comfortable, cuddle up with Maria, and we'll be in Skopje in no time at all."

He smiled, and said gently: "Not Skopje. Trieste."

"Trieste is out, Vito Glabianco is dead."

He stared at me. "Dead? Oh my God." He said grimly: "Murdered?"

"No. He had a heart attack while he was overdoing it with a beautiful woman. A lesson for you there, wouldn't you say?"

"Goddammit. That was the only lead we had."

"To what? Or to whom?"

He said, angry again: "To a man who calls himself Agathon."

"Oh, him. Well, we'll find him, in the course of time. His real name is Otho Kolettis. That makes it easy, doesn't it?"

He stared at me and I climbed into the car, waited till they both settled down in the back, carefully backed out from under the embracing shrubbery, and pointed the Jensen in the direction of the dirt road that led to Skopje.

I couldn't get the thought of Anna Obrenovic out of my mind.

CHAPTER 6

Fenrek's stamina is astounding, ever to me.

Just a short while ago he had been as close to an unpleasant death—is there any other kind?—as a man can be, and now... Now he was sitting up in the back of the car enjoying the ministrations of his lovely lady. It was almost as though he enjoyed the pain and the anxiety because they would, in turn, bring all that motherly, hen-fluttering attention from her.

And then, suddenly, for no apparent reason, he was babbling incoherently. He raised his voice and shouted: "Goddesses don't cry, do they? So where did her tears come from, will you tell me that?"

I could sense the alarm in Maria. I said quietly: "It's all right, don't worry."

He suddenly switched to Hungarian and shouted: "Damn you, who the hell do you think you are?"

In the driving mirror I saw him raise his fist as though he were going to strike out at Maria, and I slammed on the brakes, hard. But suddenly, he subsided, and when I swung round he was staring at me, his face whiter than ever. He said: "What...what the devil was all that about? Oh my God!"

"Just take it easy. All right now?"

"Yes. Yes, all right. I'm sorry about that."

"You know what you did? What you said?"

"Yes. I know." He fell silent for a while, and finally reached out and patted Maria's knee with all of the old affection. "Just bear with me, my dear. Seems I'm still a trifle sick, what a bloody bore."

I said firmly: "Sick or not, you've got to tell me the prologue to all this."

The green mountains were flashing by us, bright and cool in the morning sun, the peaks standing up high, the broad valleys below us dotted with little white houses and weather-worn clapboard farm buildings, widely spaced out, as though, in this quiet and remote corner, everyone had all the land he could possibly need. The vast panorama of it stretched on three sides below us as we climbed up the steep, steep mountain.

He said, sighing: "Prologue? The wrong language, this is Yugoslavia, not Greece. But I grant you it's high drama."

"So tell. What happened after you left Maria in the Delage?"

"Ha! That beautiful car! But it won't really do much more than eighty miles an hour, and we were obviously in for a chase on a road we couldn't get off, no chance at all in eluding them." He was beginning to gesticulate fiercely, the old Fenrek coming back to life. He said: "I saw a Citroen station wagon coming up on us, and we lost it on a bend, and it seemed to me that it wouldn't be long before they'd catch up with us." He was fine again now, the spasm of near-insanity gone.

I thought I'd help him along with his little love affair. Not that he needed it. I said: "So you decided to face them on your own, without Maria?"

He beamed and patted her knee, and said to her, in a sickening sort of way: "I couldn't let you face that sort of risk, my dear."

I grimaced. "A Hungarian gallant. Go on."

"Well," he sighed, "what was I to do? They saw me standing by the side of the road and nearly skidded off it in their surprise. But they stopped, backed up furiously, and just sort of...stared at me. Then one of them jumped out and said: 'All right, get inside.' So I did. Largely because he was sticking a pistol in my belly."

"Did he know you by name?"

"Yes, though I didn't find that out until later, and I won't lose continuity, so do you mind?"

"Go on."

"Once in, the back of the Citroen, somebody very neatly and

efficiently hit me over the back of the head, and I passed out. Next thing I know, a man was bending over me with a hypodermic. I hate needles, so I struggled a bit, but... Well, I was thoroughly trussed up, ready for the spit. And then coming and going all the time, in and out of coma. I don't know what it was they gave me, but..."

I said: "I told you, so you should know. Diethylbarbituric acid, the symptoms can't be mistaken. And it surprises me a little. It *can* act as a truth drug, but that's not its prime use, and any half-competent doctor would have known that. But then, they didn't have a doctor, did they?"

"How can you be sure of that?"

"The scars they left on your arm are too ugly. An amateur with a needle, they're murder. Have you any idea what it was they wanted to know? How much do you remember?"

He snorted: "That damned stuff seemed to work half the time, and the rest of the time just made me violently ill. I found I could fight it to a certain extent, and so I did. They were trying to find out how much I knew about Agathon, though that's not what they asked me. They asked what I was doing out here, who I was after. I knew that they must know this already, so it seemed easier to go along with them, pretend that damned drug was really working efficiently." He broke off and said moodily: "Or perhaps it was working, how can I be sure? I pretended to be in a coma most of the time; but some of the time, I really was. It...came and went, you know what I mean? The only constant thing was that I felt absolutely lousy, all the time. I didn't know what the anesthetic was, I assumed it was sodium pentothal, and it worried me. I didn't want them to get carried away and pump my body full of it, so...I told them what I thought they might already know. After all, I'd been making inquiries about Agathon from the Greek, the Bulgarian and the Yugoslav police, it was quite likely they'd already know that."

"I thought you never considered likelihoods as being very rewarding phenomena?"

"Shut up, and let me talk. If I'm going to die, I may as well fill you in as much as possible."

"You won't die. You're not the type."

"My skin's on fire."

"It'll cool off. Go on."

"Well, two or three times I really did pass out, and sometimes I just faked it. A lot of the time I lay there and listened to them talking, mostly in Greek or Bulgarian. I gathered that they wanted to know how close I was on Agathon's trail, and most of all if I knew exactly what he was up to." He shrugged. "I told them repeatedly that I was working in the dark. Whether or not they believed me, I just don't know. Perhaps not. Once, one of them said they ought to be using sodium pentothal, and where could they get some? I had thought that's what they were using." He was still a little incoherent, but recovering fast; he's that sort of man; *nothing* demolishes him for long.

The morning sun was bright and cheerful, the mountains glorious. We passed by a roaring waterfall, very close to the track we were on, and I said:

"Why don't you take a rest for half an hour, some fresh air under the trees?"

The top of the car was down, of course, and we had all the fresh air we needed; but it's a strain even to sit in a speeding car when you're as sick as Fenrek was; and I wanted him thoroughly relaxed.

He said: "No, let's get on," and Maria said firmly: "We'll stop, and we'll sit under the trees for a while."

I pulled off the road and helped him out, and we went over to where the spray from the falls was not quite reaching us, a rainbow arching through it, and lay down on the fragrant grass; a lot of wild basil was growing there, and we could have been on a picnic if we'd had a few watercress sandwiches.

He lay back and stared up at the sky, and Maria leaned over him with a worried look on her face, and I said: "Don't worry about him, he's indestructible."

Fenrek said, beaming: "That's true. Quite indestructible."

I said: "Did you get any of their names? Nice if they weren't all faceless."

"Yes. One of them was named Stavros, but that's a pretty common name. He seemed to be the man in charge. About fifty-five years old, five foot nine, a hundred and sixty pounds. Black moustache, sallow complexion, brown eyes, black hair, a rather hooked nose, bushy eyebrows, the lobe of his left ear larger than the lobe on his right, very thick fingers, a gold ring with an embossed scorpion on it on the little finger of his right hand, what else? Oh yes, I got his fingerprints."

He reached into his pocket and took cut the fine silver cigarette case in which he keeps those abominable black cheroots that he always smokes when I'm not around to stop him.

He said: "They had taken this away from me, but once, when I seemed to be cooperating very nicely, I asked for something to smoke, and the man Stavros gave it back to me." He handed me the case; wrapped in a handkerchief, and said: "No gloves on, very careless of him."

"Only because they thought you'd never leave there alive."

"Yes, I suppose you're right."

"Damn right, I'm right."

I said to Maria: "Do you have any face powder? The old-fashioned kind?"

She stared at me. "No, just pancake."

"That'll do."

Mystified a trifle, and determined not to ask why, she handed me her compact, and I scraped a little of the packed power off the top with my pocketknife, and let it lie in the sun on a piece of paper to dry out. I went and got the puncture-repair kit from the Jensen. Fenrek was watching, and when I came back and sat down, he sighed and said: "Oh, God save us from the experts."

I dusted the silver case thoroughly with the dried powder, blew it all off lightly, and examined the beautiful fingerprints that were left behind. "A scar across his right thumb, how come you didn't notice that?"

Fenrek said nothing, but shook his head a little sadly.

I peeled the white backing off three of the rubber puncture-patches, and pressed them carefully over the fingerprints, lifted them off, put the backing on again, and gave them to Maria.

I said: "Next time we get a chance, send them off to Special Index, find out who this Stavros is."

She tucked them away in her purse, saying: "*Tiens, tiens*, how come they never taught me that at the Interpol course? I'm supposed to be Grade Four A, I should know about that."

"Learn a little something every day, you'll be a better woman."

Fenrek said moodily: "Stavros, not a very nice man. I told him once to go to hell, I thought I was perhaps appearing too cooperative. For a moment or two he just sat there, as though he were determined to do nothing in anger, but only after mature reflection. And then he began to beat me. I was far too weak to offer any sort of resistance, and he went on beating me till the pain was...almost insupportable." He grunted. "Casual, disinterested brutality, it's the thing I hate most of all."

"Yes, I know. What about the others?"

"There were six or seven of them all told, and one of them was a radio operator. They had a short-wave radio, did you know that?"

"Yes, I saw it. Quite a good set, a Grundig transmitter-receiver, the kind the German police use, long-range and very efficient."

"I only once heard him addressed by name, and they called him Nikko. A Greek, about twenty-eight years old, five foot four, a hundred and thirty pounds, fair hair, grey eyes..." He said suddenly: "How long was I there?"

"Two days."

"It seemed longer."

A fallow deer came hesitantly out of the thicket, its head with the broad, palmate horns held high, and stared at us for a while, and then trotted calmly down to the stream to drink. We watched till it suddenly took fright and galloped off, and I said to Fenrek:

"What can you remember of what you heard? It might be very useful."

He nodded. "That's exactly what I was thinking, I'm trying to see if... They talked, once, about their H.Q., but there wasn't much to go on."

"Whatever there is."

"Yes, I know." He was frowning horribly. He stroked his chin and said: "My God, I've got to get a shave, I can't stand it like this."

I went and took my Norelco from the case in the back of the car and tossed it to him, and he smiled at Maria and said: "Mind if I shave in your boudoir?"

He sat up and began to run the shaver over his face, and said:

"There was an occasion when one of them said: 'This damn stuff isn't working, why don't we do something about it?' The man who answered said: 'We ought to move him to H.Q., he'd be safer there, anyway.' I was just coming round from a bout of complete coma, and I don't know how long they'd been talking. They started to quarrel and one of them said,—how did it go? He said: 'No, he's a lot safer here, believe me, I never did like that place, can't think why he ever chose it.' Stavros was there, I remember, and he got very angry and said: 'Gravena chose it, and for a change, he was right. Anyway, they're moving out soon, out of the village and up to the hearth, it's only seven kilometers.' Someone asked: 'What hearth is that?' but Stavros didn't answer him. He just stared moodily out of the window and said at last something that sounded like: 'Athene's tears...' Does that make sense to you?"

The little bells of memory were ringing, the memories that spring to life if just the right word is spoken, the right sound heard, the right scent smelled. It seemed terribly important to know...

I said: "Were they speaking Greek?"

"Yes, they were."

"And the word they used for 'hearth' was *Hestia?*"

"Yes, of course." He waved an airy hand and said: "Yes, I know, Hestia was the Goddess of domesticated fire, and Athene, Athene was the daughter of Zeus and Metis, the Goddess of wisdom, and where does that get us, I wonder?"

I said: "It just might get us where we want to go. *Hestia* is the crucial word here, and we're not thinking of the goddess now, but of the ritual embers of the fire which were carried from place to place, in ancient Greece, to symbolize the continuity of the family. And Athene—we're talking about the legend of Paris and the golden apple, of course."

Maria was hanging on to every word I said; this was her world, her age, even.

I said: "When the young Paris, son of the King of Troy, gave his golden apple to Aphrodite as the fairest of all the goddesses—and merely because she opened up her gown to let him see her body, if you remember—then both Hera and Athene, the other two goddesses in the contest, went off in a sulk. Athene took with her the *hestia,* or ritual fire, and languished for a while in the mountains above Ardea. Today, there's an obscure cluster of rocks, which is about all it is, known as Athene's Hearth, two thousand feet up in the mountains of Macedonia, just over the border from Yugoslavia. Nothing but three huge boulders, smoke-stained from an ancient volcanic eruption, but they really do look like an outsized cooking hearth."

The irritation was seeping over Fenrek again. He said impatiently: "How come I've never heard of it?"

I said: "I don't suppose even Maria has, and it's her own home territory." She shook her head at me, and I got up and started to do some push-ups, I like to keep active, and I'd been doing far too much sitting still in the car lately.

I said, pushing up and down: "And you won't find it in any of the guidebooks either. You'd need a thousand volumes to list every ancient historical site in Greece, there are just too damn many of them for listing."

Fenrek said, grumbling: "All right. 1 don't like it too much, but all right. What about Athene's tears?"

"Oh, that. There's a small spring nearby, bubbling up out of the rocks. Warm, slightly salted water. That's what they call it—Athene's Tears."

He brightened up again, and I didn't like the sudden changes of temper; you can never be sure what the barbiturates are going to do to a man. He said: "Well, if your historical facts are right..."

"I don't even *mention* facts unless I'm sure of them, you know that."

"...then there ought to be a village seven kilometers down the mountain from this place. Who's got a large-scale map?"

I said: "There's one in the car, but we don't need it. The village is called Evropos. Not much of a place, really, just one main street on the edge of the cliff; and a few scattered villas in the mountains around. Seven kilometers, precisely, down the hill from the *hestia*."

He was carefully blowing the dust out of the shaver, smoothing a hand over his face and gently touching the dark, livid bruise under his eye where Stavros had beaten him. I noticed that the hand was trembling still, that he was trying to force it to hold steady and not succeeding. Maria knelt in front of him and held up her compact for him to look into, and he touched the white thigh where she had ripped open her jump suit. He said: "What a pity, I always liked that suit. Perhaps we can run up to Paris one day and get another one."

I was finishing off the push-ups, two hundred of them, and I got to my feet and said: "The hell with Paris; we're going to find a doctor, in Skopje."

Fenrek said: "The hell with the doctor too."

"Sure, once he's taken a good long look at you."

"All right, all right, if you insist."

As we walked slowly back to where the car was parked, he looked at me shrewdly and said: "Now tell me why we had to stop here."

"Oh, I thought you needed a rest, is that a good reason?"

"Not really. There's something else, isn't there?"

I felt it would be fitting to allow him his little pleasure, the pleasure of knowing he'd guessed right. I said:

"There were six men in that house, and it's fair to assume that at least one or two of them will have recovered by now from indispositions that were purely temporary. And they had a radio transmitter, remember? They'll be hard on our heels, or ahead of us by now."

He sighed: "You really do like looking for trouble, don't you?"

"No, not particularly. But if it's there, I like it to be where I can see it. So, I thought we'd give them a little time to catch up with us."

He looked askance at Maria, and I said: "Don't worry, I'll take care of her. I'll take care of you both. You're in rather better hands now, both of you."

He shook his head and took a long, deep breath. "There's no other word for it, Cain. You really are a sonofabitch."

"But such a nice fellow at heart. Climb in."

We got into the Jensen and set off, refreshed and enjoying the clean mountain air, to see if they were lying in wait for us.

They were.

CHAPTER 7

To find the tarmac road that leads to Skopje, we had to make a wide geographical detour to avoid the inhospitable and trigger-happy Albanians on their heavily-guarded frontier, so we skirted their border, taking the valley of the Beli Drim river. This is some of the wildest country in Europe, the most primitive—and the most alarming.

Here in the valley, the Serbs, and the Montenegrins, and the Herzegovinians, and sometimes the Bosnians and Magyars too, have been fighting each other for eleven centuries. And although they are all united today as subjects of one country, Yugoslavia, the old enmities persist in the rural areas; the mountains frequently are the scene of a kind of feudal banditry that no government has ever been able to control. You can travel the length and breadth of the whole country in absolute security today, but every cave, every copse, every cluster of jagged boulders still seems to conjure up the image of violence. It's something to do with the rugged terrain; here, the beautiful forests of Bosnia have changed to the harsh and fearful grandeur of the north Albanian Alps, cut with deep gorges and. frightening precipices. The waters of the rivers no longer scintillate in pretty little streams and pleasant, tree-shaded waterfalls; they rush down from the high mountains with a fury all their own, carving their own courses in the hard and weathered granite.

We drove fast, very fast, through scattered, isolated farms, and up into the hills where there was snow high above us, and the trouble came as we approached the little country hamlet of Gusinje.

I'd been stopping every once in a while to study the road ahead of us and the empty surrounding countryside through the glasses, the wonderful Leitz Trinovids I always carry in the car. Far and away the most expensive glasses in the world, but by far the best too, and there's nothing like good equipment to give you a sense of superiority, even if it's purely illusory. And now, I made a detour, forcing the Jensen over territory even a mule would have had difficulty with, climbing higher and higher to get a good look at the road, if you could call it a road, that lay ahead of us.

On the way out from Serigrad, whichever way we went, we would have to pass through one or another of five deep mountain gorges, and this was one of them. Here, anything might happen, and a certain caution was called for.

He was fast asleep on the back seat, Fenrek; the reaction had set in, and the drowsiness which I expected to follow his exposure to the drug had quite taken over. Maria was beside me in the front, and I left them there in the car while I climbed to the top of a peak that would give me an uninterrupted view of the valley below, of the gorge itself which we would have to cross. There were only two bridges here, I knew; one at Gusinje itself, and the other some four miles to the west of it, very close to the Albanian border.

I lay on my stomach and used the Leitz Trinovid binoculars to sweep the vast expanse of broken country that lay below us on the other side.

I saw the cars at once. Here, all you can logically expect to find is a farmhouse or two, a few horse-drawn carts, maybe a truck here and there, widely scattered in the empty desolation of a primitive and very rural wilderness.

Gusinje lay right below me, a small cluster of houses built in white stone, a fine old Byzantine church, two small cobbled streets, a maze of charming, trellised alleyways and courtyards; a bright little oasis on the very edge of the gorge, the river's water rushing by a hundred feet or more below it. The bridge there was timber, perhaps two hundred feet across. And in the village itself two cars were strategically parked, both out of sight of anyone driving through. One was a Jeep station wagon, carefully tucked away in the space between two buildings, and the other was a long wheelbase Tatra which had been placed very close to the wall of the church. A few people were moving along the two streets; but they looked like local inhabitants; an old man hobbling on a stick, two women with baskets on their hips, a couple of kids kicking a football around.

In the far distance the other, older bridge seemed quite deserted. It was built of stone, beautifully arched, and about eighty feet above the river. The road leading to it was overgrown with weed, seldom used since the new bridge had been put in at a more favorable point for the village carts.

From this high vantage point, and through these marvelously efficient glasses, I could see every detail, every chisel-mark in the bridge stones; I studied it for a long, long time before returning to the car.

I looked at Fenrek, snoring now; respiratory trouble, one of the effects of barbiturates when they are carelessly administered; his right arm was twitching nervously. I said to Maria: "All right?"

She was worried. "We've got to get to Skopje, to a doctor, fast."

"But we've got to get there in one piece. If I were stopping a fugitive from Serigrad, this is where I'd do it."

"But surely—we're fifty miles away now!"

"Five bottlenecks leading out of the general area. This is one of them."

"There was no telephone in Serigrad."

"No. A short-wave radio."

"Oh."

"We'll swing around Gusinje, there are some strangers in town, at least two carloads, and it's hardly a tourist area. We'll take the old bridge. Once we're over that..."

I backed the car up on the narrow road, the precipice dropping down on our right for a thousand feet or more, and drove slowly back to where I'd seen a track leading up over the mountain. It wasn't an easy drive, but the Jensen's double power train pulled is nicely up and we were over the top with nothing but a dented sump and a few scratches on the fenders, and then we were bumping down the other side, onto a deeply rutted gravel road and on beyond the village.

Here, we were lucky. The road went through a high cutting

that shielded us from any curious observer, the sandstone and granite rocks towering high on both sides of us. Ahead, the bridge was a little over half a mile away.

I still didn't like it. We were just *too* vulnerable.

I left them in the car again, and walked on ahead to scout the lay of the land. At the end of the cutting, there was an open space some hundred yards across, with weeds three feet high interspersed with bright scarlet poppies waving brightly in the breeze, a picture of rural charm and lonely beauty; and there was only silence. I crawled carefully in among the weeds and lay there on my belly for five minutes, waiting, watching, listening.

Nothing.

Nothing, that is, except a small car parked fifty feet from the bridge, close by the edge of the gorge, very close. It occurred to me that from up at the top of the mountain, where the logical approach was, it would be invisible; indeed, up there, it had been well out of my sight, concealed by a single red rock that rose up out of the roadside at the edge of the cliff like a phallic emblem. It could be coincidence, of course, that it was parked so that it could only be seen from down there, from close by, when it would be too late to do anything about it if someone were crossing the bridge and... And what?

A man was bending over the raised hood, and all the time I watched he just stood there, fiddling at something in the engine; or pretending to. I watched him through the glasses for a while, so clear and sharp now that I could see every line on his face. A small, dark, energetic sort of man, with not a single spot of grease on his hands. Interesting. I watched him doing nothing for a while longer, seeing that he looked back towards the approach road once or twice, and yawned a couple of times. Well, if he was bored, maybe we could do something about it.

I went back to the car and said to Maria: "They've set a little trap for us, bless their hearts. We're going to run right through it. Nothing like speed when you have to go somewhere fast. Get in the back with Fenrek, lie down on the floor; keep your eyes shut; and hold tight."

Her eyes were wide, and she looked at Fenrek. I said gently: "The worst we can expect is a burst of machine gun fire. At best, a couple of rifle shots. But we'll be travelling fast. Just hold very tight." I thought it would be unkind to tell her of the explosive charges I'd seen in the Serigrad house; after all, the deduction that *plastique* was the weapon they'd be using was no more than a likelihood, something that any protégé of Fenrek's never really believed in.

And now, the four-wheel drive and the immense American mill of the Jensen were about to pay their way. A four-wheel drive British chassis, an elegant Italian body (now sadly marred and not looking at all its splendid best) and above all, the startling get-up-and-go of the overhead valve 6-1/4 liter engine. I put my foot down hard and the car shot forward like the charge of an angry water buffalo. With three people aboard (and my own weight is over two hundred pounds) the standing quarter-mile takes fourteen seconds, which is a mite better than the Ferrari, and at the end of that time we were doing a hundred and two miles per hour. It's like being shot out of a cannon, and we hit the narrow stone bridge, with two inches or so to spare on either side, at a hundred and twenty-five, the radial tires, Michelin XAS, sending up clouds of dust and debris as they bit into the weed-grown, gravel surface.

There was no machine gun, no rifle even. Instead, the whole bridge blew up behind us as we hit the other side. I felt the hammer-blow of the *plastique* as it caught the end of the car and tried to up-end us, base over apex. But we were simply travelling too fast; bow do you deflect a cannonball? I heard the drumming of rubble on the rear bodywork, and some small pebbles came showering down on us, and I heard Maria scream. I yelled: "All right?"

She yelled back: "All right, my God!"

I took my eyes off the road long enough, one split second, to see the man by the car with his hands still on the plunger. He was looking over his shoulder at us, startled half out of his wits because we were still rolling, and I thought it was fitting to do something about him.

I braked hard, and swung the wheel over savagely, and we went off the road and circled round, missing the edge of the gorge by an inch, and then I drove the Jensen straight at him. Maria, not entirely to my surprise, was sitting up and screaming again as we headed at fifty miles an hour for the very lip of the precipice. I saw him leap away, reach into the car and drag out a rifle—what a hopeless gesture!—and then try to jump clear as he saw it was too late.

It was one of those comic little Citroen *deux cheveaux*, a tiny, two horsepower runabout made of sheets of corrugated aluminum, the ugliest car in. the world, possibly the cheapest, and certainly one of the most efficient, a light-weight toy that will go *anywhere*. Right now, it was going over the edge.

He changed his mind again, not a very bright man, and threw up the rifle to his shoulder. Did he think he was going to stop a charging, powerful brute of a car with a rifle bullet? I yelled to Maria: "Down!" as the shot went off. It didn't even go near us, because, as he fired he tried to leap aside. But he was too slow. The needle of the speedometer had gone past the sixty when I hit him, driving him into his little toy car, and then I hit the brakes hard, and the Jensen just stopped where it was, dead in its tracks. But first, it just barely touched the little Citroen, one billiard ball striking another. And the little car went sailing over the edge, rolling over and over down the steep incline. It didn't even burst into flames; those things carry a gas tank not much more capacious than a good Zippo.

I got out and inspected the damage. The Jensen's front wheels were precisely on the edge of the cliff, not an inch away, not an inch over. There was a nasty scratch on the front bumper, and one of the headlight glasses was cracked, and that was all.

I climbed back into the car. Maria sighed a deep, deep sigh, and said plaintively: "Couldn't we just take the train the rest of the way?"

I said: "You know where the cognac is."

She reached for it, drank deeply; and I looked sat Fenrek and saw that he was still fast asleep.

I backed up carefully, swung round once again, and headed for the High Alps, the road twisting and turning as we climbed up and up-and up and up, one glorious hairpin turn after another, the whole of an ancient, savage country spread out on the plains far below us. At the top, I pushed her up to eighty, and searched for the road that would take us on to Dacovica, Prizren, and Skopje.

* * *

Skopje is the only town in the world that lies in the middle, literally, of a cemetery. It's a big town for this part of the world, with a population of about a hundred and twenty thousand; the old Turkish cemetery completely surrounds it—an indication of its prior importance as the central crossing of the Balkans, fought over by Greeks and Bulgars, by Turks and Macedonians, by Serbs and Magyars, and more recently by Italians and Germans. The Vardar river runs through it, and after the harsh mountains to the northwest, it is a charming, exotic, and delightful place, with Turkish minarets everywhere, and gilt-domed mosques, and white-washed walls topped by red tiles, with heavy, time-worn timbers everywhere, and archways covered over with morning-glory and jasmine, honeysuckle and wisteria; everywhere you look, there are reminders of Macedonia's ancient glory.

It's two towns, really, built, like Buda and Pest, on opposite banks of the river that is its life-line. The left bank is modern and industrial, but the right bank is something else again—ancient, historic, and picturesque in the best of Byzantine form.

Both the great Empires founded on Constantinople, the Roman and the Ottoman, had always found it necessary to hold this area in a firm grip; the valley of the river Vardar was the easiest route from Salonika to the north, and for their conquests of the Serbs, the Bosnians, the Albanians, and the Magyars, Skopje was the center of their communications system. Even in modern history, it was the fall of Skopje in 1941 that signified Axis control, through the Germans' Bulgarian allies, of the whole of the Balkans.

But now, on the lazy right bank at least, the town is quiet, and sleepy, and at peace with the world; and quite charming.

We checked in at the Kosovo Hotel, with its balconied rooms, covered over with vines, that looked across the treetops to the beautiful Vardar.

The Doctor was a dour and silent man, who had been sent by the army in answer to Maria's request through the local police. I didn't want to take any chances with a stranger; the sight of a hypodermic in strange hands can be alarming if there's the taint of evil in what you're fighting; I was still worried about the *scope* of the opposition, and didn't want to take any risks. So they sent us a Captain from the

Military Medical Corps who was attached to Skopje's famous drug center, a man who knew what he had to do, and did it silently, quickly, and efficiently.

I suggested an injection of picrotoxin, and the doctor looked at me coldly and said: "Is it *Doctor* Cain?"

"No, just plain mister. But I know he's had an overdose, carelessly administered, of diethylbarbituric acid."

He leaned down and peered darkly into Fenrek's left eye, and said: "Yes, so it might seem." He felt the pulse, took the temperature twice, not believing it the first time, pulled out a single hair and burned it, smelling the smoke, and said at last: "It could, of course, have been Evipal."

I said patiently: "No, it could not. Evipal is n-methyl-5 cyclohexenyl-5-methyl, which makes it a short actor, even one of the ultra-shorts. This is a *long* actor. He needs picrotoxin, nothing else. Unless of course you don't have it, in which case..."

He said, interrupting me: "Would you care to wait outside, Mister Cain?"

I said pleasantly: "No, I would rather not. Why don't you just forget I'm here? And give him some picrotoxin."

He sighed and prepared the hypodermic. When it was all over, he said severely: "You will rest, Colonel Fenrek, for at least a week. For one week, you must not leave your bed."

Fenrek nodded. "Of course, Doctor. Whatever you say."

I knew that he'd be out of it five minutes after the doctor had gone.

I went to the phone and asked room service to send up a bottle of Remy Martin to celebrate his return from the edge of idiocy, and when the Captain had gone, sniffing audibly, he said waspishly: "Does he think I'm a pregnant woman, for God's sake? Who's got a map of the Greek border, and why do I have to ask for it a dozen times?"

I said: "Relax, some good cognac on the way up, we'll all have a quiet little drink together and I'll see if I need your help to push this thing through. You can tell us all about the exciting times you've been having. You're a well man again, and I won't put up with any more of your damned nonsense."

The Inspector, whose name was Krnj (which is pronounced

Krnjh in Serbo-Croat), was smiling to himself, waiting for someone to put him in the picture.

He said: "We had a report of a bridge being blown up near Gusinje. Apparently the village there was invaded this morning by no less than eleven armed men who came down out of nowhere and took up hiding places in the church, after having cut the wires of the village's three telephones. And now, a senior Interpol executive turns up, showing clear signs of battle. I wonder if there'd be any kind of connection there? So little of a truly criminal nature happens in our little country, that anything like this takes on the appearance of a veritable crime wave."

I nodded: "And moreover, there's a village up north called Serigrad, a house with a lot of high explosives and guns in its cellar, and half-a-dozen undesirables making a nuisance of themselves there. That's part of the picture too."

"Ah yes, I heard about that."

I looked at Fenrek and said, knowing how much it would discomfort him: "Serigrad used to be called Serpolis. The last resting place of a Greek guerrilla fighter named Felas Agathon."

Fenrek sat up straight, staring at me ludicrously. He spluttered: "Felas...*Felas* Agathon? Who the hell was that?"

He leaned back into the pillows and said: "My God, all this time, the only Agathon that came to my mind, to all our minds... My God, it never occurred to me that there might be another one."

I shrugged. "No good having an education, you know, if you're not going to apply it."

Maria was staring at nothing, lost in her secret thoughts.

Fenrek said, sighing: "So that's how you found me."

"I'm surprised you hadn't asked me that before."

He grimaced. "I was waiting for you to ask me why I *didn't* ask you. I can't outwait you, can I? Ever."

"Nope."

"Did I thank you for saving my life?"

"I don't suppose you did. I don't remember. I only did it for Maria, anyway. I've got to help you keep the girls happy, haven't I? But I'm glad I had the chance, I got to meet a Princess, a charming, delightful woman."

I saw Maria looking at me a trifle suspiciously. I said to Fenrek: "Tell me about your Agathon."

He was furious that he'd been misled for so long by the mis-association of names. He punched his pillow and said: "All right. We learned in Paris that a man whose code name was Agathon, a Greek guerrilla from ELAS, the old terrorist organization, had turned up alive, though he was supposed to be dead. That was four, five months ago, and since that time, no more reports that he was even still alive. Then, there was a particularly brutal killing in Florina, in Northern Greece, some people named Crespos killed for no apparent reason at all, and Agathon's print was found on the bloodied tile floor. Now, Crespos had apparently just left a truck driver named Jablanica, and this Jablanica was almost, but not quite, a witness to the killing."

Krnj nodded. "I remember the case. It was reported to Interpol as a matter of routine, because Crespos was a foreigner, from Greece."

One of those little bells was ringing in my mind, I said: "That's twice in the last couple of days I've heard the phrase: *a particularly brutal killing*. All killing is brutal. What was special about this one?"

Krnj said: "He was horribly mutilated, He was castrated, both his hands were cut off at the wrists, and both his feet at the ankles. Finally, he was disemboweled. And nobody even heard him scream."

"Gagged?"

"No sign of gagging. Our reconstruction suggested that his brother arrived during the torture, and was killed at once. And that his wife and sister were both killed some time later when they returned from the cinema."

"And they were tortured too."

I didn't make it sound like a question, and he looked at me shrewdly and said: "Yes, the wife was, quite, terribly. The sister simply had her throat cut, apparently while she was trying to get away. Her body was outside the kitchen, where the others were, as though she'd tried to run to the front door and had almost made it."

"Rape?"

He sighed. "Yes, the wife. After she was dead."

"Nice people." I said to Fenrek: "Special Index presumably checked on Crespos?"

"They did. Nothing. No known history."

"Fingerprints?"

"Neither by his fingerprints, nor the Bertillon System. As far as Interpol is concerned, he had no criminal background, under that or any other name."

I said: "What about Klaus Cernik?"

He frowned: "Who is Klaus Cernik?"

"Just another part of the puzzle. We'll get to him later. There's a pattern emerging, isn't there?"

Maria said slowly: "But it's not a very clear pattern, is it?"

"Not yet. Just a few ideas at the back of my mind."

"I wish you'd share them with us." When I did not answer, she dropped back quietly into that strange, introspective daze that was part of *her* pattern.

In the silence, Krnj broke wind. He glared at nothing in particular, and mumbled something, and Maria came out of her mood and laughed softly.

Fenrek said hastily: "Most of the time, they talked Greek, I pretended I couldn't understand it."

I said: "Very easy for you, your Greek is lousy."

He ignored the comment and went on: "The old trick. He said, in Greek, talking casually to one of the others: 'Does he know we killed the girl he was running around with?' I was quite sure it was a lie, to find out if I knew what they were talking about, and I kept a perfectly straight face. After that, they talked more freely in front of me, but I'm afraid I didn't learn very much."

"And there's no reason to suppose that Agathon himself was one of your captors?"

"None."

"What was it that Vito Giabianco was supposed to tell you, have you any idea at all?"

Fenrek sighed. "The name of a man in the Trieste jail who is a little highlight on the Agathon scene."

"Splendid. We already know who that is. Klaus Cernik."

He hated gathering in threads that were not of his own weaving. He said: "Can we be sure?"

"No, we can't. But it's a likelihood, at the very least. Klaus Ceraik was captured while fighting with ELAS in northern Greece, in the mountains near Evropos..."

"Ha!"

"...and has been flitting around the world, under various aliases, ever since he escaped."

"How do you know that?"

"We checked with Special Index."

"Good. Now tell me why?"

"Because Cernik was in jail with your Jablanica's uncle, who is a pianist. Just before the uncle was released, Cernik crushed his hand to a pulp by stomping on it. Obviously, a warning to him not to talk to you or anyone else."

He grunted. "That's a very tenuous sort of connection, wouldn't you say?"

"Not in the least bit tenuous. The kind of connection I'm assuming would really call for the uncle to be killed off before he could do any damage by talking out of turn. But—and it's a big *but*—in jail, you cannot really murder someone and hope to get away with it. If one prisoner beats up another, there's not very much fuss made, but murder—that's an entirely different matter. If Cernik had taken the natural course and killed Giabianco, then he would have promptly been sentenced to *ergastolo*, the rest of his life behind bars. So instead, he applied just as much pressure as he thought he could get away with, a warning to keep quiet."

"And now he's dead, and we've walked into a brick wall."

"Not quite. We've lost one stepping stone, we leap onto the next one. Klaus Cerndk. But before we tackle him..." I said to the Inspector Krnj: "How long will it take to find Jablanica and bring him here?"

He smiled thinly. "Not long, Mr. Cain. He is in jail, in Titograd."

"Titograd!" Ha! the pattern really was taking shape. I said: "Titograd is only a few miles from Agathon's Serpolis, and that's a coincidence I won't accept either. What's he in for?"

The Inspector broke wind again. He looked at Maria and mumbled: "Sorry, just can't help it. Most people get used to it, in time. That's what they tell me, anyway." He squirmed in his chair and said: "A minor case. He was caught with a load of stolen medical supplies, at a routine road check. He'll be brought to trial in a few weeks, and will probably serve six months. I can bring him here very quickly."

I could feel the hair at the back of my scalp tingling. "You have a list of those supplies?"

He was watching me shrewdly, trying to get ahead of my thinking and not quite succeeding. "Yes, of course."

"Then tell me if they include, perhaps, a drug called Surital? Or procaine hydrochloride? Or thiopental sodium, perhaps? Or, dammit, even a simple barbiturate?"

The wheels in his head were turning furiously. I could feel Maria's big round eyes on me. The Inspector said slowly: "It was mostly aspirin, iodine, Mercurochrome, rubbing alcohol, gauze, bandages, the kind of stuff that could readily be sold anywhere, with no suspicion attached. But yes, there was a small bottle of procaine hydrochloride. I'm not sure, I don't think I know what it's used for."

"It's an anesthetic. Like thiopental sodium, more commonly called sodium pentothal, it can be used as a sort of truth drug. Not a very good term for it, but an adequate description. A strong likelihood, isn't it, that he was taking it to Serigrad, just ten kilometers over the mountain. They were using a simpler barbiturate on Fenrek, and it wasn't working." A thought occurred to me, and I asked Fenrek: "Correct? Or are we all exaggerating your powers of resistance?"

He shook his head. "I can't answer that. I was slipping in and out of coma all the time. What I told them, if anything at all, I just don't know. It couldn't have been very much. I don't know very much."

"Then they would have assumed you were fighting it, and demanded something stronger, something with more predictable results. So they sent for some procaine. Of course, on top of diethylbarbituric acid, it would probably have killed you, but I don't suppose that would have worried them too much once they were assured of how little you really knew. But more happily, it gives us another thread to weave into the tapestry, doesn't it? It puts Jablanica squarely in their camp."

Fenrek was frowning horribly. I have always been a strong believer in the cause and effect syndrome that so many people dismiss as coincidence. But he hates this kind of assumption; like most of his kind, he's got to have facts, and if you want to be misled, there's nothing like a few facts to do it.

He was reading my thoughts again. He said: "I hate everything about it."

"You should love it. We have Agathon, Klaus, and Jablanica, faith, hope, and charity. We've gone a long way forward in the last few hours."

Fenrek said sourly: "Yes. Towards what?"

I said: "Let's get Jablanica over here, and we'll find that out, won't we?"

He scowled. You can't convince some people, even when the truth is staring them in the face. He said: "Pooff. The kind of professional tough we're up against—he won't tell us a goddam thing." He glared at Krnj and said: "You have some sort of objection to sodium pentothal over here, don't you? What's the easiest way around it?"

The Inspector squirmed his arse around uncomfortably. "Under certain circumstances, it's possible to get a Court Order. But it's not easy, I'm afraid. You have to put up a much stronger case."

I said: "What's more important, none of those truth drugs really works predictably. But we don't need it. If you want someone to talk to you, all you have to do is make sure he's doing what he thinks is right, for one reason or another. It's pretty simple, really."

Maria was smiling. She was picking up Fenrek's habit of reading my mind. She said, prompting me quite unnecessarily: "That's a tight little family, the Giabiancos, isn't it? Very tight."

I said "Exactly."

Krnj farted again.

CHAPTER 8

You will sometimes see that the older peasants of Serbia and Montenegro wear on their headgear a little strip of black silk.

They are still in mourning for the last of the Serbian kings, the great Lazar, who was killed by the Turkish Sultan Murad at the battle of Kosovo in the year 1389. And the name Kosovo implies, to the Serbs, all that is great and heroic in their history. Nearly five hundred years later, when the Serbs finally defeated the Turks on the same plain of Kosovo, the legend is that they knelt and kissed the bare earth, and that where their blood fell, bright-red peonies sprang up.

I thought of the legend now, sitting on the wide, cool balcony, with the fields of peonies in the distance beyond the white stones of the Turkish cemetery.

They had brought the truck driver, Jablanica, here with a great deal of misgiving and reluctance. They had wanted me to talk to him in the local police station, where he could be properly held in a cell; but I had insisted, and the Inspector had finally, and grudgingly, given way. He was in the bedroom, very worried, guarding the door, and two more policemen were on the hotel grounds; we sat together on the verandah like old friends, I with a glass of cognac, and Jablanica with a bottle of slivovitz sent up from the bar.

I let him sit there for a long time while I studied him. He was an angry-looking man, much younger than I'd imagined, with a quick and volatile temper; impetuous was the word that came first to my mind, and I thought this might be turned to good advantage. He was very powerfully built, with a flat, tight stomach and heavy shoulders, his forearms bulging under a tight blue sweater. He had the Giabianco family nose, and a disconcerting habit of glaring fiercely at everything in sight. I had to keep reminding myself that he was an Italian, not a Serb at all. He sat a wooden chair on the balcony, backwards, his chin resting on his folded arms across the chair's back, and glared down into the garden where the two policemen were.

When he realized that I wasn't going to start talking until he settled down a bit, he grumpily drank from the bottle, in great, greedy gulps, shaking his black unruly hair away from his forehead after every swallow.

I said at last, very carefully: "Your uncle in Trieste, Vito Giabianco, was supposed to know something of interest to the police, and we went all the way to Italy to see him. It seems that all you told them was that Vito was somehow connected with the people who slaughtered the Crespos family in Florina. Now, I want to know two things. First, just what that connection is, and secondly, what was it that persuaded you to talk to the police in the first place. Are you prepared to answer those questions freely?"

He pushed his chair angrily away, a sharp, incisive movement, and stood up to grip the balcony rails with both hands. He spun round suddenly to look at me, and said coldly: "No. I am not."

It was strange how very much spur-of-the-moment his movements were; it was as though he always made up his mind instantly, and then charged in with no further reflection.

I said: "Will you at least tell me why you were carrying a bottle of procaine hydrochloride to Serigrad?"

He turned his back on me and said: "A bottle of what?"

A question is always better than a straight refusal to say anything, particularly when a man wants to hide his face when he's talking.

I said: "Procaine, it's a kind of anesthetic."

"Oh, that." He turned back, his features composed now, and said: "I've already admitted to the police that I broke into a pharmacy and helped myself to some stuff I thought I could sell. I didn't know what it all was. I just took what was handy."

"Aspirin, iodine, that sort of stuff?"

"Yes. That sort of stuff."

"Plus one bottle of a potent and very dangerous drug."

He shrugged. "I didn't know what it was."

"The police tell me you have no criminal record. What made you suddenly turn thief? For a few hundred dinars' worth of medicines?"

He grinned. "We all make mistakes once in a while. I'd parked the truck in the alley behind the store, and I noticed that the window was half-open, so I went inside to see what I could find. I didn't stop to think about it very much." I said nothing, and he waited a while and shrugged again, and said: "If I'd stopped to think, I suppose I wouldn't have done it, but... Well, I figured I could make a few dinars easily, and these were very hard times for a poor man."

"Yes. Hard times for all of us." I let it hang there, taking my time, plenty of time.

It's impossible, of course, to rely absolutely on first impressions, but I'm not often wrong in my estimation of a man; and there's no sense in having good judgement if you don't put it to work. I was quite convinced that this surly and impatient young man was just not a natural villain, and the question he couldn't—or wouldn't—answer had been a very important one. What makes a simple and honest man suddenly turn petty thief?

Either he wasn't so simple, or so honest. And yet, I'd told Fenrek *he's in their camp*, and I knew that I was right. Temporarily, then? Against his will? Or was my appraisal of him all to hell and gone? I didn't think so.

I said: "Why were you carrying it to Serigrad?"

The name did not faze him anymore, he was ready for it. "Serigrad? I don't even know where that is."

"Just the other side of the mountain from the road check where you were picked up."

"Oh. I've never been there."

I switched tracks. "You know, of course, that your uncle is dead?"

His eyes dropped. "Yes, I heard about that. What a hell of a way to die. He was a good man."

I was reminded again of the tightness of the Giabianco family, a family of rough and gentle people who thought in terms of dignity and honor, a close-knit clan who lived for their music and for nothing else. And here, the youngest of the clan, an honest truck driver turned small-time thief for no accountable reason.

I said: "Yes, a very good man, I was with him when he died." I wondered if it might be the slightest touch of a bond between us. Was he coming, very slightly, over to my side? Of course not. But I knew now where I had to hit him. But change his trend of thought for the moment, and come back to that later. I said: "Tell me about the Crespos murder."

"You must have seen the reports, I told the police everything I knew, at the time. I haven't learned anything since then."

He was talking more freely now, an arrogance asserting itself. As soon as his assurance was complete...I said: "Go over it again."

He sighed, and sat down again, and took a drink and said: "I'd been to the concert with Stefan Crespos, and had driven home with him in his Opel. It wasn't running very well, and I promised to fix it for him. As I was driving away, oh, maybe a hundred yards or so up the road, the timing went off completely, and I stopped to fix it. It took me a long time, because I didn't have the right tools, and as I was standing there, I saw four men coming towards me, in a hurry, and it seemed to me that they'd come from Stefan's house. I didn't think anything of it until the next morning, when I learned that...I learned that the whole family had been wiped out. I knew then that the men I'd seen were the murderers, and so I tipped off the police."

I said drily: "A good citizen? That sort of thing?"

"No!" It was an explosion of anger. "Stefan was my friend, a good man, and they butchered him!"

"Was he as close to you as your own family?"

He almost snarled at me. "What the hell does that matter? He was close, very close."

"I was just remembering how closely knit the Giabiancos are, that's all."

He stared at me suspiciously, sure that something was going on and not liking it because he couldn't understand it. He put the conversation back on its track: "The police called in a young Greek lady, the lady in the other room, and then that guy turned up, said he was from Interpol, and..." He shrugged. "That's about it."

"How old are you, Giabianco?"

It surprised him. "Twenty-eight. You've seen my dossier."

"And Stefan Crespos?"

"You've seen his too, what is all this?"

"Just answer the question. It's hardly a deathly secret."

"He was about forty, a little less maybe."

In the room, through the open French windows, Krnj announced his continuing presence with a continuing rumble; Jablanica looked shocked.

I asked him: "What was it your uncle knew that he was going to tell the police?"

He'd said enough, too much. His mouth closed up like a clam, and he shook his head. Was it fear? Or just the determination of the very young not to cooperate too closely with the establishment?

It seemed important to remember that he had no way of knowing that whatever was going on in Serigrad was connected, very decidedly, with Stefan Crespos' murder. But not quite time to make the point yet; I knew too little, too. I said: "Give me the connection, Giabianco, between your uncle and Stefan Crespos. That much won't hurt you. And you might derive comfort from what I have to say."

He stared at me, puzzled, then said vaguely: "Oh...I just thought my uncle might have some idea who the murderers were."

"Oh? How come?"

"Before my uncle went to jail, he used to hang around a lot with Stefan Crespos."

It was an easy way out, and there was a possibility that it was true.

I said: "What was the concert you'd been to?"

He shrugged. "The State Orchestra was visiting Florina, a Polish violinist, I've forgotten her name, she wasn't that good. But they'd hired Stefan as her pianist, her own was down with the flu. I was in town, on my way to Salonika with a load of machine tools, and so I went along with him. Got in free."

I found it remarkable that no one had ever bothered to mention the fact that Crespos was also a pianist; but then, why should they? I was quite convinced that this young man knew a lot more than he was prepared to say.

And so, it was time, now, to hit him.

I said idly: "Apparently you believed the story that your uncle died from a heart attack?"

He stared at me. "Of course." His dark brows were furrowed, and there was a very angry look on his face. He said belligerently: "What do you mean, *'the story'?*"

He suddenly thought he'd found the truth, and he blustered and said: "My God, are you saying...?"

I waited.

He was furious now, and he took a long swallow of slivovitz and said tightly: "I think you'd better tell me what's on your mind." He was right on top, aggressive and demanding, glaring at me and waiting for an explanation.

I said, lying easily: "We put out the story that he died of natural causes for our own reasons. In actual fact, he was shot. A bullet from a rifle, fired from the rooftop across the street, through his bedroom window."

His eyes, his mouth, his whole face was open wide. The impetuosity had all gone, because now he just didn't know what to do, which way to leap. He snapped his mouth shut and said, spitting out the word: "Cernik!"

"No. Klaus Cernik is in prison, in Trieste, in the same jail your uncle was in."

He just stood there, staring, almost in shock. He picked up the slivovitz bottle and held it, looking at the label, and then, suddenly, spun round and hurled it down into the garden where one of the two policemen was standing. It hit him in the small of the back, and I saw him swing round and aim his rifle in an instinctive gesture, and I called out urgently: "No! No, it's all right!"

Inspector Krnj was suddenly there beside us, alarmed and angry. "What happened?"

I said: "Nothing. He had a bit of a shock, that's all I just told him his uncle was murdered."

He didn't know what I was talking about, but he frowned and said: "Oh, that." Under the circumstances, it was the best thing he could do.

Jablanica sat down on one of the wickerwork chairs and sunk his head in his hands, and I said gently: "You were hoping that your uncle would help us get your revenge on the men who killed your friend Stefan. Now he can't. So it's up to you."

He just sat there, breathing hard. He said at last, heavily: "Yes. Yes, now it's up to me. All right, I'll tell you what you want to know. Just...ask the questions."

I said: "Just talk. And keep on talking."

"Well..." Krnj was leaning against the door to the bedroom, arms folded, waiting.

Jablanica said: "Well, in the old days, when I was a kid, my uncle used to play with Stefan. He wasn't really that good, my uncle, he never made it as a pianist, and Stefan, well, Stefan was a sort of child prodigy who took up with him. We'd sit and chat after their playing. I was sort of the link between them, if you know what I mean. And Stefan told us once that, when he was a child, he used to hang around in the mountains with a terrorist group named, I think, ELAS, a popular front, you know the sort of thing. Just a kid, but he used to run errands for them."

It figured. In the old days it was part of the pattern; seven year olds were the best messengers they had, kids too young to be suspect.

"That was up on the Serbian-Greek frontier. Well, there was a Colonel named Klaus Cernik who kind of took Stefan under his wing, because Stefan brought him food and wine one day when he was badly wounded, carried it right through the government lines, saved his life. He became their sort of mascot."

"Their mascot? Who were the others? What were their names?"

"I don't know, I've forgotten." He said irritably: "Does it matter?"

"Yes, it matters very much. They're the people who killed your uncle."

He frowned darkly, and thought for a while, and said, mumbling: "Hell, it was a long time ago that he told me, I don't know... One of them was a Colonel, Stavros or something, and the other was a civilian named something like Marathon."

I did not prompt him, and he looked at me and said: "Or was it

Agathias?"

I said: "Try again, Jablanica."

He shook his head. "No, I can't remember."

"And this was in the early nineteen-forties?"

"About then. Anyway, Stavros and this...Marathon or whatever his name was, just about ran ELAS between them, and..." He broke off suddenly and said: "Another one was called Gravena, I remember. Marathon, Stavros, Klaus Cernik, and Gravena. Then the whole organization got broken up, the war was over and the revolution was over soon afterwards, and they all split up, and then..."

He sat there, brooding in silence for a long while, and then said: "I threw my bottle away, didn't I? It was still half full."

I leaned over the verandah and called to the policeman down there: "Anything left in that bottle?"

It was lying on the ground still, the policeman waiting until it could be picked up discreetly. A little ruefully, he retrieved it and tossed it up to me, and I pulled the cork and gave the bottle to Jablanica. He took a long drink and said:

"Then, it must have been, I don't know, ten years or so later, Cernik turned up again. He'd been in a fight, and he turned up in Florina, where Stefan lived, with a bullet hole through his throat. Would have killed a normal man, Stefan said but he found his way to the Crespos house and Stefan fixed him up, no doctor, Cernik wouldn't allow it. Apparently he thought he was dying, he was sure of it, because he gave Stefan...I don't know, a list of secret numbers, or something. And then Stefan was called in by the police, because they were looking for someone who'd shot his way through a roadblock, but they released him, because Stefan kept quiet, of course, and by the time be got back to the house, Cernik was gone. Never saw him again."

I said: "What were those secret numbers? What did they represent?"

He shook his head: "I don't know."

There was an awful gap in his story.

I said: "When I told you your uncle was killed, you said: 'Cernik!' Why, if they were such good friends, if Stefan had twice saved his life? It doesn't make much sense, does it?"

Now he was getting angry again. He said: "I don't give a damn whether it makes sense or not. All I know is that in spite of all that, Stefan was terrified that one day Cernik would turn up and kill him. And Uncle Vito knew *why*, I'm sure of it. Hell, I heard him say it once: 'Vito, if I get myself killed in an accident, tell the police it was Klaus Cernik, he's a brutal, sadistic man.' I remember it well, because my uncle only laughed and said: 'I tell them the whole story; they're going to be very rich men, aren't they?' And then...then they were both laughing about it." So when he got himself butchered like that, I sent the police to Vito in Trieste, it was the least I could do."

Everything was falling neatly into place, not too tidily, but nicely. I said: "What about your trip to Serigrad? It was Serigrad you were going to, wasn't it?"

He sighed. "Yes, it was, though that was nothing to do with the Crespos business." He looked at Krnj and said: "All right, all right, I smuggle cigarettes once in a while, up into Albania, get a good price for them there. A lot of people know that, and when I was passing through Titograd, a fellow stopped me, a stranger in town by the looks of him, a strong Bulgarian accent, and said he wanted some medicine in a hurry. It was nighttime and the pharmacies were closed. He seemed to know all about me, mentioned the names of a couple of people I've bought cigarettes from. He offered me fifteen hundred dinars for the medicine, which is a lot of money, I could hardly refuse, could I? More money than I make in a month. I told him, just don't bust into a pharmacy like that, you've got to find the right one, the right time. He said to meet him on the road outside Serigrad at four in the morning." He said glumly: "It was two-thirty when they stopped me and found all that stuff."

"How did you know what to look for?"

"He wrote the name down on a piece of paper for me, procaine something or other, told me I'd find it in one of the locked cabinets. I found it, knocked the cabinet over and broke it to make it look accidental, and took along some aspirin and stuff that I could sell over the border. They're short of medicines over there."

He looked at Krnj again and said: "I'm talking my head off, aren't't I? Is that going to help?"

Krnj nodded: "It will mitigate very considerably in your favor."

He glowered. "Not me. I mean, will it help to find the men who killed my uncle? It won't, will it?"

Krnj broke wind again, and frowned, and Jablanica said impatiently: "That Serigrad business, it doesn't mean a thing. I'm more interested in Cernik's head. No one's going to murder my uncle and get away with it."

I didn't have the heart to tell him I'd fed him a mess of lies: that could wait. Instead, I said: "The same people, Jablanica. Crespos, your uncle, Serigrad—the same people. And you were helping them."

"Oh my God!"

"The wheel keeps turning, all the time, doesn't it?"

He looked at me long and hard. He said slowly: "You know, in these parts the Serbs don't think too highly of life. But I'm an Italian, really, and for us it's quite different, it means a lot more to us. And when you get Cernik—I want to be there. Yes, the wheel keeps turning."

Krnj said affably: "Be there? You'll be back in jail, my boy. But it won't be too bad, I promise you."

They took him back to prison, a young man with a load off his shoulders, and left me alone with Fenrek and Maria. I brought them up to date on all that Jablanica had told me, and we carefully sketched out the picture that was slowly, but inexorably, emerging, and at seven o'clock in the evening Krnj came hurrying back, all his affability gone, a terrible scowl on his face now.

He said, the moment I opened the door to him: "We've just had word from Sezana, the frontier post near Trieste."

I was sure I knew what was coming.

He stormed in, the only word for it, and glared at Fenrek and said: "Four men killed, machine-gunned, four of the frontier guards."

I said: "Cernik, without a doubt."

"Yes."

Maria was trembling. She poured Krnj a drink and took one herself, and he gulped it down like vodka, and ran a hand through his bushy hair, and said:

"Four men, just doing their duty, the whole country's after the killers." He put down his glass and sighed and said: "Forgive me. We don't often have this sort of thing here, it's...unnerving."

Fenrek said: "Yes, I know. What happened?"

The heat of the day had gone, and there was a cool breeze coming in through the wide open windows, bringing with it the scent of honeysuckle; I could hear the buzzing of a bee on the verandah, searching out the sweet stamens. A hummingbird, a bright red flash, darted into the room and hovered, staring at us, then darted out again.

Krnj said: "Four o'clock this afternoon, a heavy truck crashed through the frontier barricades at Sezana. I don't know if you know the place, it's at the top of a long hill, a good field of view down into the Italian side, where there is merely a painted wooden bar across the road. Our men saw the truck crash through it, and there was an Italian police car chasing it, a mile or two down the road, so they turned out quickly with their guns ready, rifles and pistols, you understand, though we wouldn't use them so close to the border except in an emergency. Anyway, the truck came on, crashed right through our own barrier, demolishing it completely, and when one of the guards fired a single shot at its tires, two men poked their heads out of the back and opened up with Bren guns, killing four of the men and wounding one other. They have no transport at the post, so the wounded man got on the telephone, but by the time he was able to get through..." Krnj sighed, "They'd disappeared into thin air. The Italians, meanwhile, drove up. Our relationship there happens to be a very good one, and unofficially they came over the border and told us that a man named Klaus Cernik had broken out of the prison in Trieste, taking four other men with him, using guns that someone had apparently smuggled in to them. They asked for our help, of course, and an official request will no doubt be forthcoming. But meanwhile, Cernik and the others are somewhere in Yugoslavia, heading God knows where."

I said: "The truck? Not many roads up there, it shouldn't be too hard to stop it."

Krnj shook his head, a tired and angry man "They found the truck, not fifteen kilometers up the road. A woodsman who was making charcoal there said he saw a helicopter land and take off with five men from the vehicle. His charcoal was exploding..." He broke off and said: "You know how charcoal sounds like rifle fire when it's burning? They apparently thought he'd fired at them and fired back with a machine gun. Three bullets, in his legs, one in his chest, three in his shoulders. A tough old Croat, eighty-years-old if he's a day, with seven bullets in him, tearing him apart. He'll live, but four of our frontier guards are dead, and that's something I won't sit still for."

Fenrek said: "The Air Force?"

Krnj nodded: "They've been alerted, but do you realize how hard it will be to spot a helicopter flying low in those valleys? And if they cross into Austria, or Hungary, or Romania, Albania, Greece, Bulgaria, or back into Italy—that's the trouble with this country, we've seven borders to police, just too many frontiers."

His bowels were giving him trouble again, and he squirmed and looked at Fenrek and said: "Call your office in Geneva, they want to talk to you, it's urgent."

Fenrek nodded. "All right. And why don't you get in touch with the Greek police? About your fugitives?"

Krnj squinted. "You think they're headed for Greece?"

"Yes. A place called..." He looked at me and said:

"What was the name of that village?"

I said: "Evropos."

CHAPTER 9

Fenrek was as bright and alert as he'd ever been, with just the bruises on his face as a reminder that only a few hours earlier he'd been very close to dying.

He sat on the edge of the bed and put the call through to Geneva. He wore a towel around his waist while the hotel people were cleaning his clothes, and we heard Maria singing softly to herself as she took a shower, the bathroom door carelessly open.

As we waited for the call, I said: "I spoke with London while you were out of commission. Thought you might like to know someone tapped the line while we were talking."

"Oh my God. You know how difficult that is to do, with the Rossier system?"

The *Systeme Rossier* is a new telephonic service that some of the major police departments, and Interpol, are just starting to use.

I said: "I know."

"I felt from the very beginning that there was a leak of some sort in H.Q. It's quite unheard of, in all our history..."

I interrupted him: "Not *all* your history. Need I remind you of Herr Heidrich? Or Daluege?"

It is not often remembered that Interpol—known in its early days as the International Congress of Criminal Police—was once under the brutal hand of the man who was to become Czechoslovakia's Gauleiter (who met a sticky and much-deserved end in Prague); and subsequently under Daluege, who was Himmler's predecessor. That was in the bad old days when the Nazis had taken over Austria and Interpol had been moved to Berlin. It didn't last too long.

Fenrek grimaced: "In *recent* history."

"Is that why you didn't tell Political what you were up to?"

He sighed. He hates it when I go snooping around behind his back, even when it's vitally necessary. He said: "Someone stole Agathon's *Portrait Parle* from the files, and that's unheard of too."

"But, of course, there was a microfilm copy of it in Geneva."

"Of course."

"And whoever the thief was, he was the man who put Stavros and the others on to you."

"Presumably."

"Then we'll have to find him, won't we?"

He said grimly: "We'll find him."

The call came through. He picked up the phone and identified himself, and waited for the voiceprint check. Suddenly, all his grumpiness went, and there was an alert, even excited look on his face. He said quickly: "Has she been stopped? No? Good, don't let her know she's suspected."

He listened for a while, and then said: "All right, this is what we'll do. You'll have to arrange for the plane to stop in Skopje. Yes, that's right, an unscheduled stop. How full is the plane? What? All right, put a man on the plane and see that he gets the seat next to her, and gets off at Skopje. Can you manage that, you won't have much time. Good. Give me her description."

He listened for a long while; they're very thorough over these things at Interpol; by the time he was through he'd have every detail of her body, down to the length of the left little toe. He said at last:

"Now, she may have taken a ticket to Salonika to throw us off, of throw someone else off, so if she leaves the plane before then have the man follow and keep in touch with you, is that clear? Good. I'll take it from there."

He gave them his precise whereabouts and rang off, and I said, chiding him: "No scrambler, if the line is tapped you're in trouble."

"I know, and I hate it. But sometimes, that's a risk you have to take. The bank robberies I was looking into..."

"Ah yes, I wondered when you'd tell me about those."

109

"There were three of them—Larissa, Paloviv, and right here in Skopje. The bank guard in Larissa was a retired cop, a detective, and he'd been trained in the Bertillon system of identification. One of the robbers answered very closely to the description we have of Agathon. A very old description, but as you know, the Bertillon index doesn't change much with age. So, I came out to take a look. And now, some of the stolen currency has turned up in Switzerland."

"Ah! I like the sound of that, very much."

He looked at me strangely, but refused to ask what I meant; sheer pig-headedness. He went on: "Some small bills. We wouldn't normally have the numbers and she'd feel perfectly safe in using them. But one of the hundred-drachma bills had the teller's identifying mark on it, she'd just been counting out bills and had scribbled her signature on one of them. Positive identification."

"And someone bought herself a ticket to Salonika."

"A certain woman named Helen Poulardis, twenty-seven years old, five feet two, a hundred and two pounds, auburn hair, green eyes, very expensively dressed, a woman who describes herself as an actress, they're checking on that now. A singularly attractive woman, by all reports, on her way to Salonika. And I will take the vacant seat on the plane beside her, and insinuate myself into her confidences."

Maria was just coming out of the bathroom, a towel round her tight little body, looking very desirable indeed, rubbing her hair with another towel, tossing it back from her face in that very appealing gesture of femininity. She said: "Whose vacant seat are you going to take?"

I said firmly: "Nobody's." Fenrek started to object, and I said: "An extremely attractive young woman has turned up with some of the money from the Larissa bank robbery, and he wants to get cozy with her. We can't allow that, can we?"

Maria looked highly indignant, and said nothing. But Fenrek exploded. He said angrily: "Good God, what are you talking about? She's the only lead we've got!"

"I'll go and see her."

He pulled up short and stared at me, and then sighed and said, reading my mind; as always: "Ah yes, if she's tied in with Agathon, she just might know me. A photograph, a description..."

"She might even have seen you in the Serigrad house while you were in one of your fancy comas." Maria was smiling gently at me, and I said to her: "Do you think you can handle the Jensen? Fenrek drives it all the time; but in the state he's in..."

He said coldly: "I'm perfectly well, thank you."

"You're not. Until you're out of incubation, you'll be getting the shivers once in a while, and I prize that car far too much to risk it. Maria, on the other hand, used to own a beautiful old Delage, and so..."

"*Used* to own?"

I suppose he was assuming she'd garaged it some place while she was with me. I told him it had been blown up by a grenade that was meant for the Jensen, and he looked suitably shocked and promptly told her the Department would see she got a replacement. I thought: wait till his accountant in Paris hears about *that!*

He said grudgingly: "All right, we'll go to the airport and drop you there, and then Maria can take the car on to Salonika. We'll meet at the Metropole Hotel, and then...then what?"

"Then we go on to Evropos."

"Good, so let's get on over there. Flight seventy-eight from Geneva gets into Salonika at ten-forty-two, so the touchdown in Skopje ought to be about ten o'clock. If we leave now, we'll have time for a drink at the airport, just in case we never see you again."

I chose to overlook that remark.

Fenrek's description did not do her any justice at all.

She was slight, petite, extremely well-groomed, and quite beautiful. The hair was amber rather than auburn, the eyes hazel rather than green; her hair was piled high on top of her head, the eyes very large and heavily-lidded with that sleepy sort of look that, sometimes, can be quite fascinating. They were very slightly slanted, and I wondered if there were some Turkish blood in her, the blood of the old gypsies who came to these parts eight hundred years ago from the steppes of Asia Minor.

There was nothing of the gypsy about her now, however. She wore a very expensive dress of dark blue knitted silk, very sensible for traveling, cut loose at the neck so that it hung in folds over a splendid breast, rather like the fashionable dresses of ancient Greece. She turned to me very coolly when I sat next to her, looked me up and down and then averted her eyes. I'm used to people staring at me, of course—my height is sometimes an embarrassment; this time, somehow, it was the sort of look that establishes a potential contact right away, an indication of a receptive frame of mind that she was obliged, for the sake of the decencies, to mask. But not too much.

When we were airborne, a young and bubbling-over stewardess came along and asked if I would like an aperitif. I said: "Some cognac, please," and the woman next to me smiled and said: "Yes, and I believe I'd like one, too."

When the drinks came along, I was suddenly very sure of what she was going to do. Goddammit, she was going to upset her glass all over me, just to make that contact; I was absolutely certain of it. So I decided to save her the trouble, and save myself the indignity of a stain all over my Brooks Brothers trousers.

I upset my glass instead, all over her lap.

I leaped to my feet with an apology, took out my handkerchief and started dabbing at her, and the stewardess clicked her young tongue and took over with practiced efficiency, and as soon as the initial burst of irritation had worn off we were almost friends.

I caught her half-laughing to herself; I'd been right, I'd just got there ahead of her.

I said: "That was terribly clumsy of me."

"Yes, it was, wasn't it?"

"I do hope I haven't ruined your dress."

"No. No, I don't think it will stain. Does it? Cognac?"

"I don't suppose so. But if it does I hope you'll allow me to replace it for you."

It was all pretty blatant, but on the other hand, she would never have replaced my trousers if she'd have gotten there first, so I didn't feel too badly about it.

I said: "At least let me have it cleaned for you."

She laughed: "Maybe I should sue the airline, isn't that the popular thing to do? And we'll split the proceeds."

"I don't believe for one moment they'd let you get away with it. Are you going to Athens?"

"No. Salonika."

"Really? So am I."

An extraordinarily attractive women, with that quite indefinable quality that somehow smothers the intelligence and pleads instead with the emotions; the kind of woman you fall helplessly in love with if you don't watch out. It's that very rare quality that drives sane men to the heights of passion or depths of despair, and it's a terrible thing to meet with.

She began looking me up and down again, more carefully, but more surreptitiously. "Business? Or pleasure?"

I said casually: "Both, really. I was sailing in the Aegean Sea last year, you know, skin diving, that sort of thing, and I found a rather valuable amphora. It finished up in the Archeological Museum in Salonika, so I thought I'd go and take another look at it. It's really quite priceless."

Her interest was rising. "A shame they make you turn these things in. A pity you couldn't have kept it."

"Oh, it would have been easy enough, I suppose, I have my own boat, I could very easily have taken it to Italy, or France, or wherever. I already have quite a collection. It wasn't really worth the trouble."

"A shame."

I said: "Is it crowded, this time of the year?" I knew that it wasn't.

"Yes, quite crowded. I'm staying at the Galerius, you'll probably find room there. It's a little too expensive to get too filled up."

"Good. So that's where I'll go."

We chatted for a little while about nothing at all, and by the time the seat-belt lights went on, our friendship, of its kind, was firmly established.

She really was a very attractive young woman, cool, poised, and very sure of herself, and I liked the way she stood apart from me at the Customs, so that she wouldn't look like a midget. People stared, of course, as they always do, and she said: "Do you ever get used to that?"

"Oh yes. What I don't get used to is banging my head on

doorways, bruises all the time."

"And you must be a very strong man."

I said earnestly: "I like to keep fit. I mean, it's all we've got, isn't it?"

She smiled. "That, and a yacht, and a priceless collection of antiques."

"Well... Anybody meeting you?"

She shook her head, looking away. It was a habit she had, her eyes were never still, always looking around. A habit? Or just a good sense of caution? "No. I'm all alone here."

"Then, since we're going to the same hotel?"

"All right. Thank you very much."

We went through Customs, and took a cab to the Galerius.

She had no reservation. We were still chatting idly together when we mechanically handed over our passports, and she was laughing about some little joke I'd made, and somehow it was all very intimate and charming.

The desk clerk handed me a key and said to the bellboy: "Take Monsieur and Madame to eighty-one." He smiled at me and said: "The top floor, M'sieur, I hope you will enjoy your stay with us."

It was as simple and as casual as it could possibly be, a perfectly natural mistake that, apparently, no one was going to do anything about.

I saw that Helen Poulardis was carefully avoiding my eye, almost giving the impression that she wasn't really aware of what was happening; and then, the Rubicon was passed, and we were both committed.

She was smiling slightly as we went up in the elevator, and when the boy had shown us the room, I said to her awkwardly: "Honestly, I didn't really intend for this to happen."

She held my look, a very amused smile on her face: "No? Then why didn't you tell him we weren't together?"

"Well..." I scratched my head, which is supposed to be an indication of idiocy. I said: "I didn't want to embarrass you, and to tell the truth...well, I was waiting for you to say it. And now, it's too late. Isn't it?"

She was laughing openly now; delighted with the situation.

She said, teasing me: "We could ask for adjacent rooms. That would satisfy them—and us."

"Them, perhaps. But...I'd rather not."

"You mean...?"

I said, terribly daring: "I wish you'd stay with me."

She gave me the necessary look that is reserved for these occasions; but thank god she didn't tell me that she wasn't that kind of a girl. She said, instead, hesitantly: "Well, the rooms are rather expensive, aren't they? All right. If that's what you really want."

She looked charming with her eyes cast modestly down. I kissed her lightly on the cheek and said happily: "So let's go down and have some dinner, shall we?"

"Just let me freshen up first. Why don't you unpack your things while I take a shower?"

She twisted round and pulled down the zipper at the back of her dress, and let it fall to the ground, and stood there holding one end of it and looking at me, and she said, very calmly: "Can we do some shopping tomorrow?"

"Of course. All the shopping you want."

"Well, that settles it all very amicably, doesn't it?"

She had an excellent figure, small-breasted, full-hipped in the Greek fashion, with long and very slender legs and the whitest skin I had ever seen.

She unfastened her bra and sort of turned away towards the bathroom, and then turned back at the door to look at me with that rather patronizing smile on her face. Patronizing, but a very agreeable-looking young woman who had the sense to know when she was on to a good thing and was prepared to make the most of it.

She said: "What are you thinking?"

"I was thinking how very lucky I am."

"Were you wondering if I do this sort of thing all the time?"

"No. Not really."

She said carefully: "It's not usually as...as casual as this. Do you know about hotel clerks?"

"Know what about them?"

"They always know at once who their customers are."

"Oh?"

"Always. You are a highly successful businessman on his first trip to Salonika, and I am your confidential secretary. This is the first time you've ever managed to persuade me to come away with you."

"Why do you say that?"

She was so attractive when she laughed! She said: "You looked like a foolish schoolboy down there. I'm sure you don't do this sort of thing very often, even if I do."

I wasn't sure I liked that.

She turned and went into the bathroom, and I called after her: "I don't even know your name."

She called back: "Helen. Helen Poulardis. Come and talk to me while I shower."

"All right."

I went into the bathroom and sat down on the toilet seat, and watched while she lathered her lovely body; and she said: "You were really planning this all the time, weren't you?"

"No. Not really. I was just, well, hoping."

"How long are you staying here?"

I shrugged. "Oh, I have no definite plans."

"Oh, the water's cold!"

"Try the hot tap."

"No. I love it. Why don't you take off your clothes, and we'll make love before dinner. You want to dry me?"

She stepped prettily out of the tub and tossed me a towel, and I dried her off and followed her into the bedroom. She laid down on top of the ornately-brocaded bedspread, a nymph among its embroidered leaves and flowers and branches, and she patted the bed beside her. She said: "Well, take your clothes off, what are you waiting for?"

I said: "To tell the truth, I was wondering how to begin."

"Oh my God. Well, there is an established routine, you know."

"Not about that. To tell you who I am."

"Ah yes, you never did tell me your name, either."

"Cabot Cain."

She said, surprised: "Cain? That doesn't sound very... But you're not Greek, are you?"

"No. As a matter of fact, I come from San Francisco, in California."

"An American! Good Heavens!" She sounded as though I had hurt her feelings, but only momentarily so. She said: "I should have known. It's not often a Greek gets to be your size, not even the mountain people. So now I know who you are. You are Cabot Cain. Come come." She patted the bed again.

I said: "And I work for Stavros. Stavros and Agathon."

I would never have believed that so much terror could appear so suddenly. One moment she was sweet and lovely and seductive, a naked Naiad waiting to be taken; and the next, there was a look on her face of the most abject fear I have ever seen. Her beautiful eyes went wide with sudden shock, her mouth dropped open, and the blood drained quite from her face. A hand went to her lips to bite off the scream, and she stared at me in complete and utter anguish.

Her voice was a whisper: "Oh dear God." She covered her eyes with her hands and started crying, and rolled over and buried her face in the pillow and kicked her legs like a child, and then she suddenly turned back and stared up at me and whispered: "Don't kill me. Please don't kill me. Please."

It was hard to keep up the pretense. I said nothing, and waited.

Now, she put her hands to her throat, covering her breasts, a terribly symbolic gesture. She stared at me, waiting for me to speak, and when I didn't, she said, whispering so quietly I could hardly hear her: "Look at me and...you couldn't kill anyone, hurt anyone who...who looks like... Oh no, dear God, dear God, dear God..." She put her hands on her breasts and said, looking straight up at the ceiling as though with a conscious effort not to read what was in my mind: "It's in a safe-deposit box, in the bank in Geneva, all of it. I just kept a few thousand drachmas, I'll give it all back, every drachma. Please don't kill me. Please?" She began sobbing helplessly, and it was as much as I could stand. '

I said, anything to get her talking: "Suppose you tell me what happened?"

She nodded, eager to please, eager to do anything: "It wasn't Gravena's fault, he banked it in my name so that it would be safer, and then—I just took it all out again the next morning and went with it to Switzerland. How did you find me?"

Was it the beginnings of a slow retreat from her fear? I said roughly: "Never mind about that. Keep talking."

"I took it out of the bank, and ran off with it, what else is there to tell?"

I wished I could answer that question. I said: "Which bank did he put it in?"

She stared at me. "Why, in Lisbon, of course, only in my name in case anyone should wonder how come he had the money. You have to show your passport when you use a safe-deposit box in Portugal, didn't you know that? So he thought it would be wiser, in case anyone asked any questions. So the next morning, while he was still sleeping off a hangover, I went and took it all out again, and skipped to Switzerland."

The next question? I could only grope in the dark at this stage. "How long have you known Gravena?"

Safe. "A long time, ever since I was sixteen years old. We weren't always lovers, but—well, you know how it is."

"I do indeed."

"I'd slept with him once or twice, but you know how he is, never satisfied with one woman. Then he told me he had to go to Lisbon for a few days, and would I come along to keep him company. He doesn't really mean anything to me." Without any trace of bitterness at all, she said: "As long as he has a bottle of *ouzo* and a woman, any woman, he is happy."

"And you really thought you could get away with it?"

"Yes, I thought that..." She broke into those helpless, desperate tears again, and said: "No, that's not true. I *hoped*, more than thought. I was frightened when I realized what I had done, but he told me that..."

She broke off, convulsed now, her tears coming uncontrollably, a terrified child with the long soft body of a woman.

I said: "He told you what?"

"He said the organization was a big one, that soon they'd have the country under their thumb, and I knew that it wouldn't be easy, not against a crowd like that, but ten million drachmas, it was more than I could resist, in my own name, just there for the taking." She stared up at me, her lovely eyes red with weeping. "Are you—are you going to kill me? Please don't. I'll do anything you want, anything, anything at all." She was imploring, desperately. I wondered how hard I could push her without giving away my own lack of knowledge.

I said: "I'll make a deal with you. I want to know more about Gravena."

Now she was completely mystified. "But you must know..." She broke off suddenly, and said: "You are a cop!"

"No, I'm not a cop. But you're guessing right, I'm not with Agathon either. Let's just say I'm a freelance, operating on my own, and that I can be just as tough as any of Agathon's mob."

"A freelance?" It didn't seem to make sense to her; she was only bright within the limits of her own little orbit.

I said: "That kind of money attracts all sorts of people, didn't you know that?"

"You mean *all* the money?"

"Of course, what else?"

"And you want..." Now the self-assurance was returning, very slowly, very hesitantly; but it was there, and I didn't like it. She said, a little breathlessly: "Can we make a deal?"

Still groping, but now I had a few answers. I said: "A deal for ten million drachmas? That's less than two hundred thousand dollars in my currency."

She took a deep breath and said: "I've got some of the digits."

"All right. How many of them? And how did you get them?"

The digits—Jablanica's secret numbers. It was all making excellent good sense now. But that assurance was getting too strong.

She said: "How safe is it to make a deal with you? What do you get out of it? And how can I be sure you'll keep your word?"

Danger, now. I said brutally: "You know what happened to Crespos? Stefan Crespos?"

She knew. The terror was back, stronger than ever; she was trembling, her white skin whiter than death with fear. It hurt me deeply to see her like this, but there was more I had to know.

I said: "I asked you a couple of questions."

She shuddered: "Gravena gave me his digits for safekeeping, in case anything happened to him. Well, not exactly that, he was drunk. Anyway, I got the second group from him, the only group he has."

"You're sure of that?"

"I'm sure. He could never hide anything from me, not when I

went to work on him. It's seven, eight, four, three." She said again: "The second group, seventy-eight, forty-three. Now you know. You don't have to hurt me. Not anymore."

The danger had not entirely gone; or gone, it could return. I said: "Don't be too sure of that."

She was pressing. She reached out and touched my knee and said: "You're not the kind to kill so cold-bloodedly."

"Perhaps you're right. Perhaps not. It would be simpler for me to get on the phone to Agathon and tell him you're here. If I tied you down, and then left, and he found you here... Is that what you want?"

Shuddering again: "No. Please, no!"

I just touched her throat gently, a terrible thing to do. I, said: "Then answer all my questions, is that understood?"

"Yes. Yes, all of them."

"Right. Start at the beginning. Who exactly is Gravena?"

"Major Georgio Gravena, a retired Army Officer, he used to be in the Greek Army."

"Back in nineteen forty-one? The time of the Communist revolt?"

"Yes, I guess so."

"And he's tied in with Stavros and Agathon?"

"Yes."

"Who else?"

"There's a man called Cernik, he's in prison somewhere. I don't know his other name."

Somewhere? The likelihood of a lie there. If she knows he's in prison, surely she must know *where?* Or perhaps not; let it ride for the moment.

"What's Agathon's real name?"

"I don't know. Nobody knows that. Just Agathon."

"All right, so far so good. Where did those ten million drachmas come from?"

"Well, Gravena and some of the others..."

"You know their names?"

She shook her head: "No. Just Stavros and Gravena, all the others were hired hands, members of the gang, no one of any importance. They held up the bank in Larissa, and got all the money, and Gravena was supposed to take it to Portugal and bank it there for safe keeping. As a precaution, because his army rank is still on his passport, he put it in my name, and we went to bed that night. I got up as soon as the bank was open, while he was still sleeping, took the money out and caught the first plane out of there, to Switzerland."

"Who has the rest of the numbers?"

"Agathon and Cernik, only Crespos knew Cernik's numbers as well, and Stavros. Five groups of four digits each."

"Five? You only gave me four. Who has the others?"

"I don't know." She was telling the truth, I was sure of it.

"And what's the sum total of the money, do you know that?"

She shook her head: "All I know is that it's the entire fund of the old ELAS operation, you remember about ELAS?"

"I remember." They'd been well financed during that long revolution. Russia, China, Bulgaria, Romania, all were sending contributions to the revolutionaries. It wouldn't be peanuts.

"And you know why Crespos was killed?"

She nodded, eager now to talk her heart off: "Agathon found out he had the Cernik group of digits. So he got it from him." Remembering, she began to cry again.

"And Gravena is still in Lisbon?"

"No, I don't suppose so." She sat up now, very slowly, as though hesitant to move too quickly, and grasped her long legs with her arms. She put her head on her knees, the long amber hair draping, and said: "I don't suppose he'd stay there once he found the money was gone. Agathon never really trusted him very much, and he'd be too scared to go back and say I'd taken the money. So, I imagine he's on his way to South America already. That's the kind of man he is."

"Well, it's fitting that the one weak link should snap the whole chain. Where's the key to the safe-deposit box in Geneva?"

"In my purse, over there."

I was looking for greed in her eyes, wondering if it would chase away the fear, or at least mitigate it a little. But there was none; the story was over for her now, and she was resigned to it. There was a terribly sad and lonely look on her face. She shrugged her delicate white shoulders, and I went and took the key, and when I sat down again she was looking at me with an almost quizzical smile of what was it? Self-deprecation?

I waited a little, and when she did not speak, I said: "I'm surprised you don't try and bargain for at least some of it."

"No. It was a dream, a nightmare, that's all."

"And now?"

She shook her head: "I don't know. If you could find me so easily, then they can too." She sat up straight and put her hands to her face. "Oh, my God. When I think of what they did to Crespos."

"You'd better get as far away as you can, as quickly as you can. Do you have money?"

She shook her head: "Nothing." In her purse there'd only been a few thousand drachma notes. I slipped off my money belt and emptied it onto the bed, about five thousand dollars, American currency, in hundreds, twenties, and tens.

I said: "Go to South America and look for your Gravena. You are not safe in Greece, anywhere in Europe. They'll find you, and they'll kill you. So run. Run fast, and far. Don't wait another day."

The terror was back on her again; it was better that way, for different reasons now. And she was trying to hide it. She hadn't even looked at the money. She said: "I'll tell you something else, something you probably don't know."

"Oh? About Cernik?"

She was surprised. "Yes. How did you guess?"

"You half-lied about him before."

For a moment she studied my face, looking for all the answers there, and not finding any. She said: "He broke out of jail, in Trieste. Now he'll be looking for Agathon, without a doubt. And he's...he's not like the others. Agathon, Stavros, Gravena—they're all savage, vicious people, and they are clever, too. But Cernik, he's different from them—he's not only savage, he's a brilliant man. And he's got his wife to help him, maybe she's as dangerous as any of them."

I said sharply: "His wife?" There'd been no mention in his PP that he was married.

"You don't know about her?"

"No. Who is she? Where is she?"

A strange and fascinating color, that hair! It seemed to sway from side to side as she shook her head slowly. "I don't know, nobody knows. Gravena used to say to me, that's what makes her dangerous, she's in the background somewhere, pulling strings, planning, scheming, always...invisible. And deadly."

"*Something* about her. Anything."

"Nothing."

"Nationality? Age? Where she came from? Where they were married?"

She said again: "Nothing. Just a wife in the background somewhere, with a reputation founded on...on nothing. I remember that when he spoke of her once, Gravena, he actually shuddered. Of course, he wasn't a very strong man, but..."

"Spoke of her? What did he say?"

She shrugged: "Something about Cernik's not being the kind of man to stay in jail, he'd escaped from prison a dozen times, always getting away, and I remember saying: 'So they'll never hold him for long in Trieste', and Gravena said: 'No, he's going to stay there, it's his wife's idea, and anything that damned woman suggests, he does, because he knows it's the best thing.'"

I thought about that for a little while, and then said: "And that, no doubt, was soon after the murder of Stefan Crespos."

She tilted her head back and looked at me, her eyes wondering. "How did you know that?"

"Just a guess. A likelihood."

"You're a strange man, Cabot Cain. Yes, it was immediately after Crespos was killed."

Like the intricate pattern on the bedspread that framed her naked body, the threads were weaving in and out, bright here and dull there, sometimes vivid and sometimes subdued, but always just where they were supposed to be.

For a long, long time there was silence between us. I felt her stir beside me, heard her long, deep breath.

Suddenly, she put out her arms to me and said: "Love me? Take me? Please? Please?"

So she *still* was not convinced. I could have wept at the pathos of it.

I said to her, very, very gently, sitting beside her very close now: "If I were the kind of man you still seem to think I am, I would not refrain from killing you merely because I'd made love to you. They raped Crespos' wife, remember? After she was dead. If I were one of *them*... You're a lovely, lovely woman, but don't depend on your beauty to get you out of trouble, ever, or that's the way you'll finish up too. No, I won't make love to you, and I won't harm you. Get out of the country as fast as you can."

The embroidered foliage of the bedspread, green and brown and gold, seemed to weave itself about her as she lay back once more and rolled over onto her side, facing me, somber and silent and sad, a naked *Hamadryade* resting among the branches of her autumn forest, but a *Hamadryade* with tears still welling up with the fear of Charon in her heart; without the silver coin, the *obol* to toss to him, she was condemned to wander forever along the desert shores and never find any refuge from her terror.

The delicate tracings of the vines were the leaves of the asphodel, the funerary plant of ruins and cemeteries.

I said again: "South America. Look for your Gravena. And don't ever come back while Agathon is still alive."

I went out and left her there, and when I looked back she was still staring at me, her eyes, dry now, sad and lonely and—perhaps for the first time in her life—terribly unsure.

I thought that no woman had ever looked more lovely, nor so infinitely desirable.

I slipped the catch on the lock to 'safe', and closed the door quietly behind me.

It was a shock to realize the effect she had on me. It was her physical perfection, and nothing else, and I knew it. But hers was a beauty so great that all sense of reason just went overboard. It was astonishing, and very disturbing.

CHAPTER 10

I walked quickly to the Metropole Hotel, through the bustling, noisy nighttime streets, the open-air cafes bright and cheerful, their patrons chatting animatedly as they took their coffee, their *ouzo*; their glasses of iced water with sweet and honeyed pastries as they watched the world go by.

A town of bright and modern aspect, but richly interspersed with the very old, all its ancient history softly floodlit. At every turning, there was a new delight. An olive tree by an old well, the red-brick grandeur of a fourteenth century church, the imposing basilica of Saint Demetrius, whom the Emperor Galerius had killed with spear thrusts, where the sacred, perfumed oil sprang from his grave through the miraculous, ancient fountain. The splendid naves of the Haghia Paraskevi, and their deep blue, fluted vases, with long branches covered with fruit, and birds, and flowers, startling and memorable against the burnished gold of the arcade. The beautiful White Tower on the broad esplanade, with the sailing boats still out on the dark blue sea behind it, the wonderfully ornate carvings on Galerius' Arch...

Surely this splendid city is one of the most beautiful in all of Europe! Even its name evokes memories of the lovely Thessalonika, wife of Macedonia's King Cassander.

The Jensen, washed and all shined up again, with only a few dents and scratches on its paintwork, was standing at the curb, and Fenrek was there in the pavement cafe, a bottle of *ouze* on the blue-checked tablecloth in front of him. Another man was with him, a short, dumpy, worried-looking man, and he waved as I went through the tall white stone archway and into the enclave. The cafe was busy with the late night crowd, and noisy beyond belief; the Greeks have a great horror of silence except during the afternoon time of siesta.

Fenrek stood up and pulled up a chair for me, and said: "There's someone I want you to meet. Captain Tsamados, of the Greek Police."

I said, as he reached out to take my hand: "From Hydra, no doubt? A famous name there."

He was blinking his eyes rapidly, looking up at me with that touch of discomfort my height seems to occasion in small men, and he sat down quickly and said: "It seems you know our islands, Mr. Cain."

"Cabot Cain. And yes, I know your islands. There was a famous Admiral Tsamados on Hydra, in the Revolution of eighteen twenty-one."

He grimaced. "How kind of you to call him an Admiral. He was, of course, a pirate, they all were." He sighed. "Ah, my beautiful Hydra. In those days, Mr. Cain, there were forty or fifty thousand people there, a great port, a great city. Today," he shrugged, "a handful of natives, and hordes of tourists."

The waiter came and brought another glassful of ice cubes, and I poured some *ouzo* and watched it take on its milky white, and Fenrek said: "Did you meet the lovely Helen Poulardis? Tsamados knows her, or knows *of* her. Apparently she was one of the children taken behind the Iron Curtain in the last days of the Revolution."

"The ELAS Revolution?"

"Yes."

Tsamados said, reminding me: "Twenty-five thousand of our children were abducted by the terrorists, Mr. Cain, and taken to Bulgaria, Yugoslavia, Albania. They were indoctrinated there, and some of them, the brighter ones, were sent back to act as messengers for the rebels. Helen Poulardis was picked up when she was eight years old, in nineteen forty-nine, during what was almost the last assault by General Papagos on the revolutionaries' stronghold, in the mountains above Evropos. She was not held, of course, so young."

"That makes her thirty years old. She looks younger. Any other record of her?"

"Nothing at all. She's known, very slightly, as an actress, very slightly indeed. She plays occasionally in the productions at Delphi, but she's not...how shall I put it? Not a person of any great consequence."

"Uh-huh." I said to Fenrek: "I can't believe Maria's in bed already."

He laughed. "Maria? No, of course not. She's gone off to church."

"Oh."

"She's one of the Anastenarides, did you know that?"

I was much surprised. The Anastenarides are almost, but not quite, pagan. Here, in the very bastion of Greek. Christianity, the old pagan cult of Anastenaria still survives, once prohibited, but now tolerated, by the Greek Orthodox Church. It's a very impressive link with Macedonia's ancient past, and the cult members claim mystical healing powers; they walk barefoot on burning embers once a year, on May twenty-first, feast day of St. Helena and St. Constantine.

Fenrek said: "She missed the feast and the fire dance this year, so she's gone off to do penance. Tell about the Poulardis woman. Did you find out where the money came from?"

"I did indeed. And it's all very simple, really. Four names. Agathon, Cernik, Stavros, Gravena. Four old-time terrorists from ELAS, now coming together again. Each of them has four digits of a twenty-digit number that opens up a bank account in Switzerland. At a guess, it's the old operating account of ELAS, which, if you remember, was quite formidable."

Tsamados was leaning forward on his elbows, peering into my face with no show of embarrassment at all. He said: "We've always believed that there must have been some hundred and thirty million drachmas, about ten million dollars in your currency. It's been lying there—somewhere—for nearly twenty-five years now."

"And if anyone presents those twenty digits to the bank, he collects the lot. That's not a bad haul to divide four ways. I wonder why they never got together before?"

Almost a conspiracy; no one wanted to ask about the fifth group. They would, sooner or later.

Fenrek shrugged. "Agathon was supposed to be dead. Without

his four digits to complete the sequence, the others would be quite powerless, and the money would have to stay where it had been put. Tantalizing."

"But Agathon wasn't dead. Why didn't he get in touch with Cernik and the others?"

"Cernik has been coming and going quite a lot these past twenty-odd years. It's possible that Agathon tried before, but was never able to catch up with him."

"It's also possible that the political climate in Greece, which has changed quite radically in the last few years, was never before favorable for what they're planning."

Tsamados said, startled: "Another ELAS revolt?"

"It's possible. Even probable. These men were fanatics, remember. Now they're all twenty-five years older, and fanaticism sometimes dies with age, but not always. They could all very well be planning a comeback."

But Fenrek said slowly: "So now, Agathon has finally found Cernik, and the ball's going to start rolling, all over again."

"No. It's not quite like that. The other way round. It's Cernik who has found Agathon."

He spread his arms, gesticulating like an Italian taxi driver. "Does it matter *who* found *whom?* The point is, they're coming together now."

I said: "It matters a great deal. The one proposition is quite different from the other."

What was it Helen Poulardis had said? 'He'll be looking for Agathon, without a doubt...' I wondered if I should have had her enlarge upon that remark. When a phrase doesn't sound quite right—if it's merely a matter of a mis-used word, a thought thrown across at the wrong time, or even, as this was, of intonation—I thought about it for a while. Was there, perhaps, an Old Terrorists Association, gathering once a year in splendid concord at some bar, wearing the OTA tie and talking about the good old days? Or would they be squabbling among themselves about who got the money?

Suppose Agathon, about whom we knew almost nothing, had been searching all these years for the elusive Cernik, searching without any results whatsoever? And suppose that, for his part, Cernik learned that Agathon had killed Crespos and thereby obtained the Cernik group of digits? Would he realize that he was going to be neatly cut out of the operation? And would he, therefore, go "looking for" Agathon?

I suspected we had a three-way battle on our hands. Gravena could be written off now—check: could he?—but we had Agathon and the Serigrad crowd on the one hand, and Cernik with his machine-gun-happy thugs from the Trieste jail on the other. And somewhere in between, Fenrek and Maria and myself, all groping blindly still; not so blindly now as before, but... And where would the denouement take place? And *how?*

I thought it might be a good idea to force one; at Evropos. But the time wasn't quite ripe. There were still a few puzzling details left, a few inconsistencies. And so, how much time did we have?

Tsamados said suddenly: "Really, I'm quite hungry. Would anyone like a pastry?"

I remembered I hadn't eaten dinner, but a pastry? The waiter was passing with a big silver tray of them, all piled high with whipped cream, *mille-feuilles* dotted with sugar and chopped pistachios and honey, and little dollops of strawberry purée. It was hard not to shudder. When I shook my head, Tsamados helped himself eagerly to three of the creamiest ones, and called for more iced water to drink with them. It occurred to me that his face was almost exactly the color of the *mille-feuilles*.

Fenrek said: "And Inspector Krnj is in town."

"Oh? Our friend with the disconcerting bowels. Isn't it off limits for him, over the border?"

Tsamados waved a forkful of whipped cream at me and said airily: "A courtesy visit, he came to tell us that your Cernik is probably in town."

It was meant to be a bombshell, but it didn't surprise me too much. I looked at Fenrek and said: "Well, that only bears out what I said, that he was headed for the Greek border."

Fenrek nodded: "But why Salonika? Could he possibly be interested in Helen Poulardis?"

"No, there's no possibility that he could find out about her presence here, it's much too tenuous an assumption that he even knows she stole Gravena's money."

"But we put a guard on the Galerius, just in case."

"Good. How did you know she was there?"

He smiled thinly: "I had Maria check with the police. They told her that you and she had booked in there together."

"Oh."

"Room eighty-one."

"Yes indeed. How strong is the probability that Cernik is here?"

Fenrek shrugged: "His helicopter apparently crash-landed in Yugoslavia, very close to the border, in a field near Miravci, on the Vardar River."

"That's very close to the railway track, the train that crosses the border."

"The first thing that occurred to Inspector Krnj. He checked with the railway people. No one seems to have seen them board the train, but that's to be expected. However, when it arrived in Salonika, two men were seen to jump off from under the last coach, just before the train entered the yards. Might have been them. Might not."

"As it crosses the border, the train passes within fifteen miles of Evropos. I wonder why he didn't drop off there, if that's where he's heading."

Tsamados was pushing a puff pastry into his mouth. He said: "It would be very much easier to go all the way to Salonika and pick up a car here for the trip back than to walk those fifteen miles over the mountain to Evropos. It's most inhospitable terrain up there, it really is. Practically impassable."

"It's more likely he's getting a few men together."

Tsamados frowned: "That's a very alarming thought."

"Uh-huh. Interesting, anyway." I reached into my pocket for the key I had gotten from Helen and gave it to Fenek: "A safe-deposit box in Geneva, the proceeds of one of those bank robberies. Helen Poulardis stole it from a member of Agathon's gang, a man named Gravena, whom I think we can now discount entirely. It seems that having lost all that loot, he'll be afraid to face Agathon. And I can't say I blame him, really. It's nice to know that at least some of them suffer from normal human weaknesses."

He took the key and frowned at it. "I never did understand the reason for those robberies."

I shrugged. "They're after a great deal more. Meanwhile, they've got to have operating expenses. That's all it represents, a supply of ready cash."

"I suppose so." He didn't sound too sure, and I said:

"Take my word for it."

"It seems a great deal of money to be called ready cash."

"He needed a great deal. He was hiding out, and at the same time tracking down the missing digits. That might entail quite a lot of traveling, a lot of time."

"And we don't, presumably, know where the missing numbers are? Who has them?"

"I could make a guess. But I won't."

Tsamados, scion of the great pirate-Admiral, had finished his disgusting blobs of goo, and was happily wiping his mouth. He tossed off a glass of iced water, finished his *ouzo* with relish, and put on his professional worried look again. He said: "Well, if there's anything else I can do...?"

I was happy to see him go; somehow, the sight of all that excessive fat depressed me, and I made a mental note to get a lot more exercise; I'd been sitting around far too much lately, and that always makes me feel bad.

I said: "Why don't we leave a note for Maria and go on over to the Athos? I'm starving."

"All right. But there's never anywhere to park in Salonika, why don't we take a cab?"

I said firmly: "We'll walk."

He sighed: "If you insist. And on the way there, you can tell me all about the lovely Helen. Is she as beautiful as she sounds?"

"Helen of Troy, Aphrodite, Maia of the fair tresses whom Cronus loved. And perhaps a little of Callisto too. Kalliste, the most beautiful of all women. Zeus seduced her, you remember, and then changed her into a she-bear to save her from the terrible jealousy of the goddess Artemis."

Fenrek hates being lectured, even in the nicest way. He said sourly: "And Artemis pierced her with a hunting arrow, none the less."

"Yes, she did. The wheel never stopped turning, even for the

Gods."

It was one o'clock in the morning when we arrived at the Athos, and it was still crowded with late-night diners. A small, nostalgic sort of place, down a few steps into a cellar, with the ceiling supported by a single Doric pillar that had been brought there, eight hundred years ago, from the Palaestra of Olympia. The cavern had been excavated after the great fire of 1917, which reduced half of the city to ruins, and the huge stone blocks that had been discovered there had been left where they were found, the seats and tables arranged around them; with the block-granite floor, it made for an overpowering feeling of antiquity, as though yesterday were still part of today, as though tomorrow were part of the past too.

We ordered some roast lamb cut from the huge upright grill at the back of the restaurant, an ancient wrought-iron piece of rococo that consisted of a single huge, upright skewer turning slowly against a background of dusty red coals, all topped off with mutton fat and heavily spiced with garlic, basil, and marjoram. They brought us some of the wine they call *retzing*, tasting strongly of the pinesap which the Greeks use during fermentation to remove, they say, the taste of the goatskin bags. Personally I have always believed that the ripe flavor of goats would be rather better than that of pinesap, but the Greeks have been doing this for thirty-five hundred years now, so I suppose we must allow them their little foibles. But the *arnaki* was excellent, and I ate hungrily, thinking about Helen Poulardis, lying there on her lovely bed. Would she be on her way already, fleeing to South America or wherever, to look for the lover she had so casually betrayed?

I also thought of Anna Obrenovic, seeing her again with the long peasant braids of her hair, waving at me as I left, standing among the green and pleasant hazel saplings.

And of Maria, too, Fenrek's Maria, who talked too much and hadn't spoken a word for such a long, long time, a strange and volatile woman who seemed to be so much in love with her boss that it was almost comic to watch. Almost, but not quite—there was something sad about her devotion, too, as though she herself were aware of its wastefulness. A great love affair going strong, for as long as they remained together, and no longer; with Fenrek, there would never be any of the passionate, desperate, till-the-day-we-die longings.

Obviously, she knew that as soon as he was gone, every time, there'd be other, all-consuming passions. What did she do in the interim? What did any of them do in the interim?

I watched him while we were eating; poised and cool and aristocratic, sharp and alert and efficient, and all in all a thoroughly good man, in every sense of the word. It was hard not to sigh for her.

I went back to thinking of yellow braids. And then of that long, amber hair; a strange, alluring color, that matched perfectly the amber tones of her skin.

And Cernik? Where was he now, at this moment? I found myself looking around the room, wondering if one of the noisy, boisterous Greeks there was our elusive Bulgarian? Was he sitting there somewhere, enjoying his *retzing*, and watching us?

Fenrek said: "You're not eating. What's on your mind?"

Before I could answer, he looked up, smiling, and Maria was there; Tsamados and Krnj were with her. The smile went from Fenrek's face, and I saw that Maria's eyes were red again, a touch of tears.

He said: "For God's sake, what happened?"

Tsamados said, the worried look gone now and nothing but anger there: "Helen Poulardis. She's dead."

I could feel the blood draining out of my face. "*Love me,*" she had said, "*take me, please?*" If I had spent the night with her, as I was tempted to... I knew that my face was white.

I said harshly: "What happened? There was supposed to be someone guarding her, wasn't there?"

And even that was their idea, not mine. I had been so sure that he'd never get to her if, indeed, there were some as yet unexplained reason why he even should. How could he have known about Gravena and the money? How could he have known she was in Salonika? It didn't make any sense at all.

Fenrek pulled up a chair for Maria and fussed over her, holding her wrist in his strong hand, offering her the comfort of his presence. The others plunked themselves down, and Tsamados said angrily:

"No, not guarding her, just watching the hotel, and that's not really quite the same thing." He pulled an envelope from the pocket of his baggy suit, and opened up a small poster. He said: "Watching for this man, Klaus Cernik, the photos came by special messenger from Italy. We had a man outside, a man in the lobby, they should have seen him. But they didn't. There's a lot of people milling around the Galerius, the best bar in town, one of the best restaurants, it would have been easy enough to miss him. But they shouldn't have done, and heads are going to roll."

He wiped at the sweat on the back of his neck, and Krnj said stolidly: "We don't know it was Cernik, do we?"

Tsamados sighed: "No, we don't. We don't even know it was murder."

Not murder?

I said: "Go on."

I felt that Maria's eyes were on me, feeling my pain. Tsamados picked up my glass of wine and drained it, and spread his arms and said:

"I'm sorry, that's yours, isn't it?" The waiter was already pouring him a fresh glass, and he drank that too and said gloomily: "No, we don't even know it was murder. But I hate coincidences. A woman under protection, in case someone tries to kill her, and a couple of hours later she's dead, would you say coincidence?"

I said: "No. Go on."

The twining vines of the floral pattern had been a counterpart to the lithe young body, the leaves the color of that glorious hair.

He said: "She was lying on the bed..."

"Dressed?"

He looked at me strangely: "Yes, fully dressed. Why do you ask?"

"How was she killed?"

"She was curled up on her side, both hands round the handle of a long pair of scissors, right through the heart. Can a woman do that? It takes enormous strength to drive a pair of scissors into your chest, enormous...endurance. At the first entry...the pain... She hadn't even unpacked her clothes, everything all neatly in her suitcase," When I'd left her, the suitcase had been open, a few things carelessly pulled out of it.

"What time was this?"

"Just before midnight. Her phone was off the hook, and they went to tell her. When she didn't answer the knock, the maid opened the door with a passkey and peered in."

"Did you ask if she'd called anyone? The Airline, perhaps?"

"We checked. No calls." He looked up at me suddenly; I was conscious that Krnj, silent and correct in his role as observer, was watching me very closely. Tsamados said: "No calls to the Airline. She couldn't have been going anywhere by air, she had no money. Just a few thousand drachma notes. Were you thinking of something specific?"

"No. Nothing." They were both watching me.

I said heavily: "I, too, prefer not to believe in coincidence. Let's assume that she was murdered. Let's even assume that it was Cernik."

I pulled the poster across the table and studied it. An intelligent-looking face, a trifle heavy, not brutal at all, but with an air of great authority about it. The eyes were very pale, which is unusual for a Bulgarian, and quite large, the forehead wide, the features sharp and aggressive. He looked like a very successful chairman of the board, except for the prison drab. Six foot one, powerfully built, born in November, 1914, in Plovdiv, Bulgaria.

I already knew his history, far more than was printed here; now, I wanted to get close to the man himself. Heavy lobes to his ears, slight, very dark eyebrows, a marked line running down the sides of the mouth, well-defined lips, a good firm jaw... I stared hard at it, trying to insinuate myself into his consciousness.

Tsamados said: "We went round to the Galerius to find you. Madame Christophorous turned up while we were looking for you, so we took her cab and came over, all of us."

I was conscious of the catch in my voice, and I hated it. I said: "The body?"

"At the morgue. There'll be an autopsy, of course, but if you want to see it before they..."

"No!" I wondered if I was shouting.

I stood up abruptly; my bones were cold, ice-cold, almost a fever. I said to Fenrek: "I'm driving to Evropos, tonight, now. You want to come along?"

He put a bill on the table, and took Maria's arm. "Let's get going." He looked: at Tsamados. "Can we drop you off at the station?"

"Well, that's very kind of you." He was suddenly a touch embarrassed, and half-smiled and said diffidently; "And I'm afraid we had to borrow some money from Madame for the cab fare. I ran out of change, and Krnj has only got dinars, they're not very acceptable here. Could you take care of it for me?"

Absently, Fenrek nodded. It didn't seem very important, but you can never tell with Greeks; inherently, they're all terribly correct.

Outside in the cool night air, so fresh after the stuffiness inside, Krnj nodded towards a taxi that was just coming up, the driver beaming. He said: "The same cab, let's take him."

The driver grinned and said, in tolerably good English: "Back to the Galerius? You don't find room in there? Or I take you some other place. I know plenty good places still open."

I said: "No, back to the hotel."

How fragile a thing is chance! If we hadn't found the same cab, the same driver, who knows how it might have all turned out. The soft and lovely *Kalliste*, the most beautiful of women, lying there on her autumn bed, pierced by the shafts of Artemis, whom the Romans called Diana, the Huntress, and no one to appease her sad and lonely ghost, no one to throw the ancient Charon his silver coin... If we had been a few moments earlier, or later, would she have been doomed to wander along those deserted shores forever?

Skin-deep, they say; and her mind was the mind of a greedy mistress-thief. And yet, beauty such as hers is both an emotional and an intellectual delight, and of these two forces, it is always—or should be—the emotion that is the greater. I knew how that for just a few moments I had been in love with her, deeply, unaccountably, and...wastefully, too.

I felt that I was trembling quite uncontrollably, and the driver chatted away as we drove back to the hotel, and at last I said irritably: "Please, be quiet."

I caught him looking reproachfully at me in the mirror, and he fell silent. I said: "I'm sorry, forgive me. It's just that..."

He nodded. "I understand, sir." His weathered old face crinkled up, and he said, grinning: "Three men, only one lady, believe me, I understand."

We pulled up outside the tall white stone archway, just behind the Jensen, and as I fumbled for my wallet, Fenrek and the others moved off to one side, talking quietly together. Fenrek was saying to Tsamados:

"We should be there in an hour or so. It might be helpful if you would come up in the morning, could you do that?"

I did not hear what Tsamados answered; the driver was chatting away at me again. I turned back to him: "I beg your pardon?"

"You are American, I think, no?"

"Yes. How much do I owe you?"

"Twelve drachmas. You do something for me?"

"Sure."

I handed him a ten and a five, and he passed me an American ten-dollar bill and said: "You tell me if this is okay, is mutilated, is maybe no good, eh? What you think?"

One corner of the bill was torn off, not very much of it, and someone had drawn a moustache and a beard on Alexander Hamilton's supercilious face, an upturned moustache and a Van Dyke beard.

I said: "No, it's all right, as long as the number is still there."

"But it is torn, is no good maybe?"

A Van Dyke beard drawn in green ballpoint. It made the great Statesman look like the Laughing Cavalier, something that, once seen, would be remembered.

I said: "Let me change it for you." I handed him a hundred and fifty drachmas and slipped the torn bill into my wallet.

Krnj was saying: "Of course, if that's what you want, I'll be very glad to..."

I never did find out what he was referring to; I was hot and cold all over, a sickness of the most terrible apprehension.

Fenrek and Maria looked at me, worried, and Maria put out a hand and touched me on the arm. I turned away, and sat in the Jensen while they went in and settled the bill.

I stared out at the brightly-lit street and thought about the Anastenarides, who walked barefoot on red-hot coals, and went to do penance at their own half-pagan Midnight Mass whenever they missed the strange and purifying ritual of the yearly fire-dance. When was it?

On May the twenty-first? The day that Persephone came back from the Underworld, when the whole of the earth could spring to life again?

Persephone... When the sweet-scented Spring came, she left the dark shadows of Hades and put on a mantle of a thousand flowers, but for the darker part of the year she slept with the God of the Lower World, Hades the Unseen, and where did her true and sad affections lie?

They were all Greeks, the Anastenarides, but Greeks who had lived over the border, in Bulgaria, and had returned to their homeland, bringing their pagan cult with them.

I hardly heard Fenrek open the door and help Maria in. I pushed the button and the engine purred, and soon we were leaving the lovely, tragic city behind us, and climbing up the steep, winding road in the darkness, the mountain road that led to Evropos; and to whatever was waiting for us there.

The Jensen's little clock was chiming half-past two in the morning.

The hills were grey and dark, the vast undulating groves of olive and fir trees lying over them like the folds of a mantle; Apollo's mantle, the poets called it. Above, as the road swung round, a white moon showed us the awesome peak of Mount Olympus, seventy miles away and still imposing its presence on us, as though the Gods seated on their huge thrones were reminding us that it was they, not ourselves, who were controlling our destinies.

We climbed up and up and up, onto the high mountains where the Earth was born.

CHAPTER 11

In these early hours of the morning, the village was dead.

It lay along the edge of a steep gorge, a single main road winding its way between whitewashed houses with curved red tiles on their roofs, a mass of strange and twisted shapes interspersed with tall dark cypresses and gnarled, ancient olives. A single rock, stark and wind-battered, towered high into the night sky, a hundred feet or more, and the village was clustered around it, the red roofs dwarfed by its imposing, stark magnificence. The thin, cold air was damp; we were at more than six thousand feet here.

Under the full moon, there were white highlights among the dark trees on the mountain slopes, the pretty little villas, well secluded; these were the homes of gentry, some of whom would come here once or twice a year from Athens, or from Larissa, or Salonika, to spend a few weeks hunting in the high mountains. Some of them belonged to the owners of the little stores here that did a handsome trade, in the summer, when the tourists came to escape the heat of the valleys. There was the smell of burning charcoal exploding in the pits.

We found the single hotel, a charming and ramshackle jumble of old white stones, tucked in a corner under the massive rock, from which a stone archway curved gently out into the street, and woke them up and found rooms. The sleepy owner accepted our apology, an eighty-year old woman who walked, bent nearly double, with the help of a stick as crooked and worn as she was. She insisted on waking her granddaughter to carry our light bags, and said, smiling toothlessly:

"My husband will pay his respects in the morning, he is drunk now."

A dark, and sweet and rather frightened young girl, sixteen years old or so, came in answer to her call, pulling a black robe hastily about her chunky body; big black eyes, and long, loose hair, and bare feet that padded soundlessly to the two rooms.

I said to Fenrek: "Go to bed, I'll see you in the morning."

"You're not sleeping?"

"No. I have some thinking to do. I'm going for a walk."

"All right."

Maria was watching me, her eyes troubled, her arms clasped about her body. All that volatility seemed to have gone, and she was quiet, withdrawn, troubled. She said: "Did she really impress you so much? Just one short visit?"

"She impressed me. Get a good night's sleep, we'll meet for coffee as soon as they're up and about, all right?"

As I turned away, she called after me: "Cabot?"

I turned.

"I'm sorry, truly sorry."

"I know. I should have foreseen it, and I didn't, it's as simple as that."

"You can't blame yourself for her death."

"I do. Good night." I could feel Fenrek's eyes burning into my back as I went down the dimly-lit hall, a wax candle burning on a small table carved from a root of olive, and down the steps and into the street.

I walked its entire length twice, a little under a mile, and found all the deserted, darkened side streets, with the smell of baking bread somewhere on the air, and then headed up higher into the hills, walking over broken ground that was strewn with boulders, with granite chips and shattered marble, with fallen pillars and great cut stones of smooth white rock, the chisel marks showing clearly in the brilliant gleam of the moon.

The cypresses were all about me, funerary and dark; I thought of Helen's asphodel, that grew along the banks of the River Styx. The night was unbelievably silent, the valley far below stretching out to the horizon and the sea, with wispy clouds of mist slowly drifting, grey against the pale blue of the sky. I heard a goat bleating sadly, and found it lying in a little hollow, its foreleg broken, and I made a stick splint with my pocketknife and fixed it with torn strips of my handkerchief; maybe it would find its way back to its herd, maybe not.

Agathon, Stavros, Cernik—where were they now? Even Gravena, could we discount him entirely?

I wandered on and on, just aimlessly wandering, moving up till I could see the village far below me, a line of tiny buildings cemented in to the edge of the cliff. I found a Proto-Ionic capital lying on the ground among the rocks, beautifully curved like the horns of a ram; a fragment of a Spartan tombstone lay nearby, and I wondered how, in all its ancient history, it had come about that it should be here. I could still see clearly the carved, seated figure, holding an amphora, two tiny figures with lyres beside it. Three slender Doric columns lay nearby, and I found that I was walking now on mosaic; there is so much of history in these mountains!

Did I know where I was going? It was hard to tell.

Across the sea to the east, and the hazy land beyond it, the sky was taking on a lighter tone, a steel-grey tinged with gold. I heard the faint bubbling of water, and found a spring; the water was salty, the salt of tears, and when I looked around I knew that I had come to the place I was searching for. The three great boulders were stained with volcanic smoke, the *hestia*, the hearth that Athene had brought here. Some idiot had drawn a foolish figure on one of the stones, in charcoal, and I rubbed it out with scrubbing sand.

I stared around, searching for—for what? I did not even know, and I sat on a broken pediment, fallen from some great portico, symmetrically carved on all sides in the manner which the Corinthians first brought here, and stared cut across the plain and waited for the sun to rise. And when it was a fiery yellow ball, gilding the sea down below, I got up and began to work my slow way back to the village.

Just below the hearth, below the salted spring, I found the marks of a tire in the loose shale. Surprising, but a very good sign.

I heard a slight noise, no more than a gentle slithering of pebbles, and when I looked round, a man was slipping down the steep slope behind me, a hundred yards or so away, a small, dark man dressed incongruously in a white business suit; he carried a rifle, quite loosely, and when he found his feet he stood there, gripping the rifle now with both hands, his feet spaced wide apart, waiting. Another man disclosed himself, stepping from behind a tall, jagged pillar of blue granite, and then a third and a fourth, and two more to my side, and at last there were seven of them, a motley crowd, some in neat silk suits, some in mountain clothes, and one, at least, in the dark-green hunting garb the gentry wear in these parts. They stood in a circle around me, not one of them closer than twenty feet, and they were waiting, so I sat down and waited too. It was a moment to light a casual cigarette, but I don't smoke, so I didn't.

I could feel the excitement rising. I pushed aside all thoughts of the lovely Helen, and forced a complete dispassion on myself; these men meant danger, and danger and passion are mortal enemies.

A tall swarthy man with a thick black moustache seemed to rise silently out of the ground no more than ten feet away. I must confess that I was surprised; I should have known of his presence there. A cave? A cistern? A flight of steps leading down to an ancient oracle?

He was slender and rather regal looking, with very sharp, alert eyes, a hooked nose and unruly hair so black that I fancied it could have been dyed. His eyebrows were straight and square, very bushy, and the tips of his heavy black moustache curled up, almost to meet his eyes. He looked like the conventional, stylized picture of a pirate—or a fanatical Greek guerrilla. And he had that indefinable air of authority about him, the poise of a leader. His rifle shoulder—he could have been a hunter out looking for mountain sheep—and his hill-villager clothes: dark woolen trousers tucked into sheepskin boots, a heavy sweater, a green woolen jacket, a hunting knife strapped to his knee.

He looked me up and down very carefully, and said at last: "A big man, a very powerful man, but you obviously won't want to make any trouble at this moment, will you?" His English was excellent, no trace of an accent.

I waited for him to sound an aitch, so I said: "You seem to have taken adequate precautions to prevent that, haven't you?"

He said: "I have indeed." It came out, very lightly, as *khave*, an almost imperceptible guttural to the aitch; Greek, then. "And there's a great deal for us to talk about, isn't there? Are you alone?"

He knew, of course. They'd been around me for a long time.

Half an hour ago I'd caught the smell of tobacco, just a whiff and then no more. I said: "Up here? Yes, I'm alone."

"And the others?"

"Back in the hotel. Still asleep, probably." I thought it a likelihood that he might know that too.

"How many of them?"

I shrugged: "I presume you already know that. Three of them. Colonel Fenrek, Madame Christophorous, Captain Tsamados."

So he *didn't* know. Well, well. They hadn't seen us down there in the village.

He was frowning now. "Tsamados too? That's a pity."

"Oh, he's not with the others. He's wandering about down there somewhere."

They'd find out that only three of us had checked into the hotel. He said: "Well, never mind. Will you come with me please?" His manner was not only courteous, it was—how shall I put it?— *weary*, as though a great fire had been there once but had long gone out. I found myself thinking he was lesser than I had expected him to be; and I knew that to be dangerous thinking.

He had turned away a little, and I said: "Not until you tell me your name, at least."

He turned back, a slight smile on his quite handsome face. "My name? I'm Agathon, of course. I thought you would know."

"There's so much we don't know about each other, isn't there?"

"And so much that we will find out. Please come with me."

Was this the man who had so brutally killed Crespos? Were those strong mountaineer's hands the ones that had wielded that mutilating knife? I found it hard to feel any enmity.

I followed Agathon up the slope, over the mosaic floor again, bright and vivid now in the early pale-yellow sun, past the bubbling spring and the dark boulders of the giant *hestia* and in among the fir trees, until we came to a narrow track, not much more than a passage for goats. Two of Agathon's men were behind me, and I fancied I heard the very slight sounds of others moving on the flanks, out of sight among the trees. We walked for five or six minutes, and then Agathon turned round to ask me a question:

"Have you seen Cernik?"

"Cernik? No, I haven't."

"I just wondered."

He moved on again, and I followed. We could have been on a pleasant, early morning stroll through the lovely woods, friends vacationing together, enjoying the delights of the hills.

Another five minutes, and we came to one of the scattered little villas, quite small and squat, a red-roofed cupola surrounded by three or four other rooms, with pleasant verandahs looking out at the mountains and the trees. There was a low stone wall around it, not much more than four feet high, and near the iron gates, open now, a young man was sitting on the wall, his knees drawn up, his arms wrapped around them, a sentry. I could see three more in the little garden; a gardener tucked his heavy revolver back into his belt and closed the gates behind us.

A delightful villa, well-proportioned more than luxurious, the sort of place an Athenian businessman would keep as a retreat for a month or so once every year, to bring his girls up here for a rest and a change of scenery. A short flight of stone steps up from the garden to the portico, nicely decorated with trailing vines. The walls were of weathered stone, the woodwork of ash, and all the windows were covered over with heavy iron grilles cemented into the stonework.

We went indoors, and Agathon stood aside for me to enter the living room, comfortable, if sparsely furnished with rather simple chairs of wood and leather with goatskins thrown carelessly over them. One chair looked extremely out of place—an old bentwood rocker that stood by itself in a corner. A very wide, high window was fitted with heavy drapes of woven buff-colored goats' hair, bordered in a brown and orange Corinthian design; they were open now, and the view across the high mountains was splendid, though the heavy iron grille gave a claustrophobic effect.

For the rest, there were a few pictures on the walls, most of them quite inferior, only one any good at all (an original Cassalis, one of Greece's newest and finest painters). But a splendid statue of the young Hermes, in the Polyclitan style, stood in one corner. I thought it might perhaps be a Roman copy from the Graeco-Roman period, probably the first century B.C. A fragment of a bas-relief showing the birth of Athena was secured to one of the walls, a priceless piece of marble, not later than the fourth century B.C. As I examined it, the two men who had followed on the path began to search me for weapons.

I said: "I never carry a gun, that's quite unnecessary." Agathon let the men continue then said: "Please sit down, won't you?"

It was all very polite and casual, and he sat opposite me in the bentwood chair and rocked slowly backward and forward while the two men left the room and closed the door gently behind them.

He said then, speaking very carefully: "The villa is very well guarded, both inside and out, you are under observation at this moment."

"I know. There could be no other reason for hanging such a terrible painting." One of the modern paintings was on scrim; the room was well lit, and if it masked a hole in the wall, which it probably did...

His eyes went to the picture, and he went on: "Outside, the grounds are full of my men, as are the hills all around us. They are armed, they know how to use their weapons, and they have been told that if you attempt to escape, you are to be shot at once. Does that put this meeting on a sensible level?"

I said: "Well, at least it indicates that you want to stay alive as long as possible."

He sighed. "Yes, indeed. I've learned to hold my life in high esteem, no doubt the reason I've managed to stay alive for so long." Was a touch of sadness there, for knowing that in his chosen work this was the one thing he could not really afford? I found it an interesting speculation.

I said: "How many men do you have, all told?"

"That is none of your business. But a very large number. Why did you bring Captain Tsamados with you up here?"

"Because if he doesn't report back in a reasonable time, they'll come looking for him. That applies to me, too, of course, and I don't suppose you want these mountains crawling with cops, do you?"

"No. Not for the moment, at least. How did you know we were here?"

"Through Stavros, indirectly. A very careless mob you had over at Serigrad."

I could see the anger in his eyes. I thought it wouldn't hurt, a little discord among them.

He said: "Yes, that's interesting. How did you find out about Serigrad?"

I shrugged. "I'm a student of history, among other things. All the facts were there for anyone who wanted to sort them out, put them all in their proper place."

He was frowning, knowing he was not on top of it all. "The facts?"

"The grave of Felas Agathon. And the birthplace of one Otho Kolettis, Agathon the second."

He stared at me, and now his anger was acute; there was a sudden glimpse, there, of the old fighting man. But he controlled himself very well, and asked the correct question: "And how long have you known my real name?"

"Just a few days. Not long enough to bandy it around in the marketplace." I didn't think it right to tell him that any inquiry after Otho Kolettis was the last thing I wanted.

"Not even to Tsamados?"

"I didn't want every cop within a hundred miles tracking you down. They get in your hair, sometimes."

He smiled, a thin, worn smile. "I'm glad we didn't come up against you in the old days, Mr. Cain. Now, of course, if doesn't really matter anymore. How much more do you know? Do you, for example, know about the digits?"

"Those? Oh yes, I know about them. In fact, I have Gravena's, the second group."

He was getting more startled by the minute. Not waiting for him to ask, I said: "Seven, eight, four, three."

He looked at me for a long, long time, and then his eyes dropped to my feet. I couldn't help the sudden feeling of revulsion.

I said: "If you think they're not the correct figures, as you seem to, let me tell you one thing. You'll never get around to hacking my feet off, the way you did to Crespos. So forget it."

He said calmly: "That remains to be seen, doesn't it?"

"I wonder if I could trouble you for some coffee. This hour of the morning..."

"Yes, of course." He couldn't have been a more courteous

host. He looked towards the scrim picture and said: "Send in some coffee, and get Stavros for me." He turned back to me: "Tell me why you are being so apparently co-operative?"

I shrugged: "There's no reason why I shouldn't be. You are not going to get away with it, you know."

Now his eyes were very sharp indeed: "With *what?*"

I said: "The ELAS fund is in a Swiss bank, what is it, about ten million dollars? To get it, you need a twenty-digit number. You have your own group, you have Stavros', and no doubt you got Gravena's before you sent him off to Lisbon. Through Crespos, you got Cernik's, and all you need now is the missing group. You're close, aren't you? But your chance of getting the rest of them is very remote."

"Oh? Who has them, Mr. Cain?"

"Suppose you tell me?"

He said again: "Who has them?"

It wasn't exactly a shot in the dark; there were bright glimmers of light there to aim at, likelihoods that had crossed the border into probability. But I had to make sure. I was certain that he knew; they'd have allocated the numbers in concord, all of them together.

I found myself thrusting the image of Helen away again. How had she put it?: *'Gravena used to say to me, that's what makes her dangerous, she's in the background somewhere, pulling strings, planning, scheming, always invisible...and deadly.'*

I said: "Cernik's wife has them." I was watching his eyes; he knew, all right. He was trying hard to keep a poker face, but he wasn't succeeding.

He said blandly: "So what makes you think I haven't got them from her?"

"If you had, you wouldn't be up here in the mountains, hiding out like a scared rabbit. You'd have taken out the funds and roused your rabble to action. The battle would have started. And it hasn't."

A lie now, to clinch things, to sew them up good and tight. I said: "Cernik's wife is dead. So goodbye to all that loot."

There was a moment of panic in those dark eyes, so brief that it was gone almost before I saw it. Well, that was natural.

But he had plenty of time to recover; Stavros came in, the man I'd kicked down the stairway at Serigrad. He stared at me with absolute venom on his angry face, and Agathon said: "Go down to the Inn, take a couple of men, bring up Fenrek and his woman. And Tsamados is in the village too, we'd better have him along as well."

Stavros transferred his gaze to Agathon: "Tsamados? We don't need him up here, he knows nothing, less than nothing."

Agathon said calmly: "Salonika will know he's here, and he may have to report in."

Stavros nodded. He looked back at me, his fury mounting, and turned his head towards the scrim on the wall and said: "Cover him, closely."

The picture swung open on its hinges, and one of the men was there, pointing the barrel of a shotgun through the square hole, a serving hatch that led to the kitchen. I braced my muscles for what was coming, and Stavros doubled up his fist and punched me hard in the belly. He hurt me not at all, but nearly broke his knuckles. He winced in pain, stood back and drove out with his foot into my groin. *That* hurt, badly.

Agathon said wearily: "Go and get the others, you can do all that you have to do later. Fenrek, his woman, and Tsamados. Have one of the men take Cain's car and drive it down the Salonika road somewhere, discreetly, don't make a fuss in the village. Then dump it over the cliff." He turned to me: "The keys, please?"

I fumbled in my pocket and found the key to the Jensen's glove compartment; that's all it unlocks, the glove compartment. I tossed it to him and said: "Just don't dent any fenders for me."

Stavros glared at me and went out. A man brought in the coffee, strong and black and thick as syrup, with half a dozen bread rolls on a tray. When he had gone, Agathon leaned back in the chair and set it rocking again. "Why did you say she was dead, Cernik's wife? I suspect you don't even know who or where she is?"

"Do you? Oh yes, you knew who she *was*, of course, she must have been one of the original leaders. But that's not quite the same thing, is it?"

He sighed, a sad old man who dyed his hair to show how young and strong he still was. "Yes, she was one of us. But she's disappeared. And now—now there's only your Colonel Fenrek to tell us where she is. You'd better all be quite sure of that."

"And if he doesn't know?"

"He *must* know!" The anger was only his desperation.

I wondered how long Agathon had been searching for her, tracking down a woman he'd known twenty years ago. Cernik had found her, found her and married her.

Agathon was sitting there, staring at me thoughtfully, rocking back and forth.

I said: "Fenrek doesn't know, take my word for it. So your mob of fanatical terrorists are going to be out of business, aren't they?"

He said again, shouting now: "He knows! I'm sure of it! They should have found out in Serigrad, *would* have found out if..." He subsided then, and said quietly: "And we are not terrorists, Mr. Cain. We are revolutionaries."

"I was thinking of the way Stefan Crespos died."

"Ah yes, that. Applied terror is sometimes necessary to all of us, establishment or...revolutionary. It serves its purpose. We need that fund, Mr. Cain, and I'll stop at nothing to get it. We need arms, arms, and more arms, and by God I'm going to get them."

I said: "You'll never overthrow the government, Agathon. Times have changed, and they're too strongly entrenched."

"No? You'll see!" He was almost shouting now, and he pulled himself up short and said, more quietly: "You can't believe that."

"What you mean is—I can't *approve* of that. But wishing the mass of the people were on your side won't put them there. They're resigned to it all, believe me."

Was he half-convinced of that himself? Suddenly he looked a great deal older. He shouted angrily: "But we can try, we *must* try!" The fury went as quickly as it had come, and he began rocking again, calming himself, a revolutionary in a rocking chair. He said thoughtfully: "What about *your* political philosophies? Do you like this bloody dictatorship, this tyranny?"

"Tyranny? A good Greek word."

Shouting again: "Yes, that's what they are! Tyrants!"

"Read your own history. The tyrants were merely the educated classes who ruled by virtue of that education. Some of them were bad, yes; but a lot of them were the best rulers Greece ever had."

He snorted: "And now? You actually *like* these Colonels?"

I said carefully: "That's not really the point, is it? I like the Greek people, that's all that matters. For four thousand years of history, you've had good rulers and bad, the Spartan totalitarians, the democrats, the oligarchs, the monarchs and the tyrants and the anarchists. My own philosophy? I don't like dictatorship, and I don't like mob rule. You're forcing that choice on the people, either the one or the other. I believe they deserve something better than both those things. And, left alone, the Greek people will find a way out...if they're really in trouble."

He said, mocking: "As they used to say in your country, 'don't rock the boat'?"

"Don't mock it. It's always the wrong people who get tipped overboard."

The anger was there again, and he said roughly: "I know what my people need."

"And you don't care how many hands and feet you have to cut off to give it to them? Who raped Crespos' dead wife?"

He was shouting again, harshly: "That was one of the others."

"Let me guess. Stavros? He seems the type."

Agathon stood up abruptly. He said: "Till your friends get here, till we can finish what we have to do..."

Interrupting him, I said: "Do you know that Cernik is gunning for you?"

He was not ready for that, and he gave himself away at once. But he said, coolly enough: "Cernik? Why should he be doing that?"

"Because he found out that you had killed Stefan Crespos, and he must have known why. So now he knows that you have his digits. He knows that when the concord gets together to withdraw all that money, he needn't even be there. He's not the kind of man to sit still for that."

"How could he find out that I'd killed Crespos?"

A search for the truth still? Was he so unsure of himself?

I said: "Who cares *how* he found out? The prison grapevine, it's a wondrous thing. And that's what your men are out there waiting for. Well, that's part of the pattern too. The old leaders at each other's throats."

My turn again. And there was one more thing I had to find out, to be sure, absolutely *certain*. The asphodel was weaving around my own throat now, tightly constricting.

I said: "Everyone assumes it was Cernik who killed Helen Poulardis. But was it you?"

There was no masking his reaction there, no masking of it at all. He said, startled: "Helen Poulardis? Dead? But why?"

"You knew her?"

"Yes, I knew her. Gravena's girl. Why should I want to kill her?"

I said: "I just wanted to be certain that you didn't."

He stared at me and said nothing.

Two of the men came in, their guns cautiously ready, and waited.

Agathon stood up and said, very calm and sure of himself now: "Fenrek will be here soon, and then we'll *know*, won't we? I'm afraid you'll never convince me that a man in his position cannot give me the answer I want, the name I have been searching for all these years. And neither will he. You might save him a great deal of grief if you tell him that, Cain. Tell him..." He broke off, and thought for a moment, and then said: "Tell him that I will show him, first, just what the extremities of pain are like. And when he has learned them, thoroughly, if he still does not break, I will impress them upon his woman. Tell him that. They say his threshold of pain is very high, but hers? I wonder? Who is she, his woman?"

I shrugged: "Just a woman."

He lit a thin cheroot, and when I went out with the two men and looked back, he was standing by the window, staring out into the warm sunlight over the beautiful mountain.

They took me to a cellar, thrust me inside, locked the heavy oak door on me and left me there.

CHAPTER 12

I had plenty of time to think, and I needed to think to pass the time; I hate being confined in a small space.

The cellar was quite roomy, actually, its stone walls whitewashed, its floor made of smooth granite blocks, its ceiling arched and very well formed, a pillar of old cylindrical stones supporting its center. In one wall, quite high up, there was a small iron-barred window, about twenty-four inches wide and some fifteen inches deep, and when I pulled myself up to it, I saw that its sill, the wall itself, was nearly two feet thick.

Opposite, in the facing wall, a locked iron-grille door separated a wine cellar from the rest of the room; the dusty bottles in their dark oak racks made me thirsty. There was an old wooden table here, a couple of discarded chairs, a sink in one corner with a single cold water tap, a heavy, empty cupboard, a carved wooden bed with leather straps for a mattress that was almost a museum piece (dating from about the middle of the thirteenth century, the time when the Crusaders overthrew the Byzantine Empire), a few lengths of good rope, a large brazier tipped over on its side, rusting, and some sacks of hazel charcoal, an assortment of pottery jars, some pieces of planking, and not much else.

But I found a piece of stiff wire and made a key out of it, unlocked the grille door that led to the wine bins, and had a look to see what they'd got there.

There wasn't very much. Mostly Greek and Italian wines of

indifferent quality, some of them not too bad, but one corner was reserved for some rather better French wines, the special occasion stuff. I found a bottle of 1961 Château Lafitte, an excellent 1964 Gavrey-Chambertin, three bottles of 1964 Fleurie Beaujolais, and more importantly, a bottle of cognac—Remy Martin Fine Champagne V.S.0.P. Not only am I very fond of good cognac, but I reasoned that it would make a passable Molotov cocktail, if I could bring myself to accept the sacrilege.

I hid the chosen supplies behind the big cupboard, and was just starting on some push-ups to keep my shoulders limber, when a man came in with a tray of food. Another man was at the door with a machine pistol poised, a German Schmeisser, and they both watched me in stolid silence for a while.

When they had gone, and I had done two hundred and fifty push-ups, I sat down to breakfast: a large flagon of good coffee, but sweetened, a loaf of excellent bread, a plate of black olives, a hunk of first-rate *feta* cheese, two bottles of tolerably cold Fux beer. (The name *Fux* is the Greek equivalent of the German *Fuchs*, and their beer is very good.)

When I had finished my meal, I walked up and down as fast as I reasonably could, and thought. As I said, I had plenty of time to do it in.

The others didn't turn up till it was nearly dark, and to my surprise there were not only Fenrek and Maria, but Tsamados and Krnj as well.

I said to Tsamados: "My God, you were supposed to be our second line of defense. I didn't think you'd arrive till after they'd visited the village. I was hoping... Well, it doesn't matter, I suppose."

He looked furiously angry, and I wasn't surprised.

I said: "I'm afraid they're going to force you to send a message to your H.Q. in Salonika, telling them that all is well, and then, no doubt, they're going to kill you. To kill all of us." I thought it wise to put them in the picture right away; I didn't want any mistaken ideas around that we'd all get out of this without a little effort.

I looked at Fenrek. "Agathon's here. He thinks you might know who and where Cernik's wife is."

He was surprised. "Cernik's wife? I didn't even know he was

married."

"Well, he is. And she's running around some place with the four missing digits, all Agathon needs to get ten million dollars out of the bank. And then they're going to finance a new revolution. Jump on their bloody white chargers and overthrow the Greek Government. ELAS all over again, with all its applied terrorism. That's something they consider to be particularly efficacious. What happened at the village?"

Maria said: "When you didn't turn up at a reasonable hour, we went looking for you. A woman in a bakery said she'd seen a man your size wandering up towards the *hestia* in the early hours of the morning, so we went looking for you there."

"We hadn't gone ten yards," Fenrek said, "when Krnj and Tsamados turned up in a taxi. We hollered, and they joined us. Half a mile from the village we walked right into three submachine guns."

Krnj was at the bars to the wine cellar. He looked back over his shoulder and said: "If there's any brandy in there, we can make some Molotov cocktails."

I said: "Just one bottle, it's behind the cupboard there."

"Oh. Then what are we waiting for?"

I said: "Just a little while longer. We need darkness."

Tsamados was glowering, his brows drawn down. "They really think I'll send H.Q. a damned message? Never. I don't care what they do to me."

Krnj said affably: "Take my advice, Tsamados, do just what they want you to do. This isn't the time to fight, obviously."

"Never!"

Krnj sighed: "Last case I can recall, they cut a man's hands and feet off. Castrated him, too. Then disemboweled him."

Tsamados' puff-pastry face was a shade whiter. He said stubbornly: "So, talking didn't save his life?"

"No, it didn't."

"Then you see what I mean, don't you?"

I wondered how far he'd let them go before they broke him; I had an idea there was a lot of courage under that flabby skin. And courage, though admirable, is not really the most useful of the virtues; it can get a man into an awful lot of trouble, when a lack of it can get him out, fast.

We waited. The light was going, slowly.

And then the door opened, and three of Agathon's men were standing there, all armed, all pointing guns in our direction. The light in the cellar was dim now, the evening outside sending its last rays through the window, filtered by the growth of vines out there, and the yellow lights behind them cast them into sharp silhouettes.

One of them said, pointing his gun at Fenrek: "You."

Fentek sighed heavily. He looked at me and I said nothing, and Maria gasped and put out her hand to him. He smiled at her and said quietly: "Don't worry, my darling, I'll be all right."

He was gone, and when the door was firmly locked behind him, I said: "All right, we can't wait any longer. Let's get out of here. Now. The window."

Krnj looked at the bars, and said: "You can't do it, that's half-inch steel."

"Not steel, it's iron, I had a look at it. But you'll have to hoist me up, I need all the leverage I can get."

"All right" He bent by the wall, and I said: "No, on your behind, I want to stand on your shoulders." He sat down then, his back to the wall, and I stepped up onto his shoulders, took hold of the two center bars with both hands, pushed my elbows out wide, and started pulling.

They were stronger than I'd thought. For a moment or two they didn't budge. Then one of them started to move, very slightly, and in another three minutes it was very decidedly bent. I reversed the process now, pushing the bars together instead of pulling them apart; as the bent one straightened out, very slowly, very painfully, the cement at its top began to crack, which is what I wanted.

I began to pull again, straining hard, and now the bent bar snapped out of its mooring at the top and I bent it back and forth till it was hot under my hands, and then pulled it down into an L-shape and swung it back and forth in the lower cementing. In two more minutes it was out, and I handed it down to Tsamados and whispered: "Two more, and we can all get through, very nicely."

Just my luck; I'd tackled the weakest of them first. It was nearly ten minutes before I had a second one out, and another ten minutes for the third. The sweat was running down my back, very uncomfortably, and I reflected again that I was getting flabby with all this inactivity.

It was quite dark outside now, and I stuck my head through and listened, and then jumped down and said to Krnj: "All right, you first, I'll lift you up. Then Tsamados, then Maria, I'll come last."

Tsamados whispered: "Fenrek, what about Fenrek?"

"I'll attend to him later. First of all..."

Suddenly, quite close by, a machine gun fired, a long, sustained burst. It was answered by the rattle of rifle fire, and then another machine gun opened up, and we heard someone scream. I said urgently:

"Get back, over by the wall, away from the window, hurry."

We were not a moment too soon. The door burst open, and the strong beam of a flashlight played over the cellar. Behind it, I could see the shadowy outlines of two men, and one of them yelled out: "No, they are all here."

In the darkness, the window was a gaping invitation to trouble. I scowled at the flashlight and said: "Turn that damn thing off, for God's sake." It held on my face, and then on Krnj, and Maria and Tsamados. I was waiting for it to sweep around the cellar and find the discarded bars, and then someone at the top of the stairs—was it Agathon?—yelled:

"Get out there, fast, they're all around us!"

The door slammed and locked and we were left alone in the darkness.

The guns outside were firing still, more angry now. One of them was quite close by, two others—was it three?—further up among the rugged stones of the mountain; the old wars being fought all over again. I heard men shouting, I heard a mortar go off, the *whissshhh* of the shell and the *thummmppp* as it exploded, close to the house.

I said: "Now they're sure we are still here, let's go."

I put a hand under Krnj's foot and he stepped up and slithered through the space I had cleared of the bars on his belly, and in a moment his face was there, and he whispered: "All clear." Tsamados pulled himself up with my help, puffing and wheezing as he tried to squeeze his belly through the narrow opening, and I wondered if my shoulders would go through. I whispered to Krnj out there: "Grab his hands and heave." The pudgy legs were thrashing, and I took hold of his ankles and shoved, and I heard him fall clumsily outside, the bushes rustling horribly as he landed.

Maria next. I said: "Hold yourself stiff." I bent down and took hold of one firm calf, put the other hand just below her breasts and lifted her up, then slid her easily through the opening, face upwards. The others pulled her through gently.

I tossed out the bottle of cognac, our only weapon, a futile one at that.

For me, it was much harder. The window was high in the wall, and though I could pull myself easily up to it, it was a question of getting the upper part of my body through; I'm not as skinny as this sort of operation would require. I reached out with one arm and took Krnj's hand and told him to heave, hard, and I wiggled myself through, and then...then we were all outside, standing in the darkness and listening to the sounds of the firing.

We could see the flashes of machineguns on the heights above us; they were using tracer bullets with a fine disregard for anyone who might see them. And why shouldn't they? Up here, in these remote passes, the closest force of the law was an hour's fast driving away, even if word could be sent—or *would* be sent—down the road from the village. I thought the villagers would all be cowering in their houses now, minding their own business, remembering other deadly battles, other times, other terrors.

Theirs was not a happy legacy; in the old revolts, almost every village here had been at least partially destroyed, men and women murdered if they showed any resistance, children carried off across the border, into Bulgaria.

Both police officers, professionally, had slithered on their bellies a little to the sides, and were staring out at the gun flashes, trying to locate them with at least some sort of precision.

I whispered to Tsamados: "Just to be sure, it's not the police or the army charging in, is it?"

He shook his head in the darkness: "No. They know nothing of all this. Colonel Fenrek wanted it all kept quiet. 'Security', he said. What are we going to do about them?"

"You know where Athene's *hestia* is?"

He frowned and thought about it. "Yes, I think perhaps I could find it. I'm not too sure."

I pointed: "Head for that peak, the one with the saddle to the left, you see the one I mean?" He nodded. "As soon as you're out of the trees, the first of the three boulders can be seen quite easily, a silhouette that looks like a man's clenched fist, the thumb sticking out. Go to the right of it, and wait for me in the copse immediately above the spring. Look for a Proto-Ionic capital lying on its side, that's where I'll come."

Krnj crawled back and whispered: "Most of them are over to the right, there must be about twelve or fifteen of them on one side, rifles and machine guns and mortars. And I think I've spotted about twenty men defending the villa, none of them near us. Will the house be empty, I wonder?"

I said: "The vital question is whether Agathon is out there with his men, or in the villa. It's a likelihood he's inside. With Fenrek."

Krnj looked at me shrewdly: "Can you justify that?"

"He has a very high respect for his own skin, but more important, he believes Fenrek knows about Cernik's wife. And that, even at this moment, is the overriding factor. He'll be in there, with Fenrek. You go with Maria and Tsamados. Leave this to me."

"No. You'll need help, all the help you can get."

I whispered patiently: "I'm better off on my own."

"No. I'm coming with you."

"You have no authority here at all."

It was a foolish argument, and he seized on it at once. He said: "Have *you,* Mr. Cain?"

"All right." I said to Maria: "Go with Tsamados, he knows where we're meeting."

Her eyes were bright in the darkness; was it fear, or excitement? She hesitated, and I knew that she wanted to come with me and had no argument at all for such a foolish move.

I said: "Go, hurry, keep very low, do what Tsamados tells you, all the way."

They moved off silently in the night; in the west, there was still a hint of pale grey light; soon it would be black as pitch.

Krnj whispered: "Moonrise?"

"We've got an hour. The battle won't last that long, it's too furious."

I broke the seals on the Remy Martin and opened it up, tore a piece from my shirt to use as a rag and stuffed the bottle's neck with it. I saw Krnj grimace: "What a terrible thing to do with good cognac."

I said: "You're a man after my own heart. Let's go."

We crept silently to the back of the house, where the kitchen was. We squirmed there on our bellies, and I touched Krnj on the shoulder and pointed. He nodded. A man was standing by the kitchen door, a rifle cradled in his hands. I gave Krnj the bottle, and signaled to him: wait.

I could hear the faint hum of a generator; there were chinks of light coming from the house, the windows not as carefully covered as they should have been, mere slits of light, far too small to see through.

Very slowly, wondering how well trained he might be, I crept up on the sentry. He was staring out at the mountains, watching the tracers that were sweeping the villa's walls now. They were uncomfortably close, but well away from the direction Maria and Tsamados had taken. A Mortar shell landed not more than a hundred feet away, and as the sentry instinctively dropped to the ground, I pounced and was on him. I drove my stiffened fingers into the side of his neck, and he lay quite still.

I ran quickly back to Krnj and whispered, my mouth almost touching his ear: "I'll take the front, give me two minutes. Then kick down the door, make as much noise as you like, I want to hear you. On the opposite wall from the entrance there's a serving hatch covered over on the other side with a picture painted on scrim. Light your cocktail, and throw it hard into the other room. Do you have a lighter?"

He nodded: "Matches."

"It won't burn very explosively, but I suppose you know that."

"A pity we couldn't have warmed it, it would have been better."

"I just need a diversion. If my guess is correct, he'll be waiting for someone to burst in on him."

He looked at me, and I said: "Cernik."

He jerked his head towards the hills, to the chattering machine guns. "That's Cernik?"

"Without a doubt. Don't forget to duck when you've thrown your grenade, or he'll blast you to hell and gone. Drop down to the floor, I want the room to myself."

He nodded and looked at his watch. "Two minutes."

Very carefully, I crept around to the front of the house, crawling among the bushes, close to the sweet-smelling earth, and when I came to the short flight of steps that led to the front door, I saw what I had been looking for: a machine gunner, his weapon mounted on a tripod; he was lying flat on his belly behind it, ready for instant action—provided it came from the right direction, in front of him, which it wouldn't. It was far too dark to see clearly, but I could make out the flared barrel and the drum magazine on top of it. Three more drums were stacked on the little wall that ran round the top of the steps. He coughed noisily while I watched him, and eased the gun over a trifle. I was closer now. I thought it might be the Russian Degtyrarov DP 7.62mm., a light machine gun, one of their favorite export items. An unsophisticated gin, 47 rounds per magazine.

I sneaked up to the low wall, vaulted quickly over it, and landed heavily with both feet hard in the small of his back. It's not easy to take two hundred and ten pounds like that, and I heard his back break. I picked up his gun and checked it out quickly; I was right, a Degtyrarov.

The timing was just right.

I was poised by the front door when I heard the sound of the back door going down, and I put my foot against the latch and shoved hard. The door burst off its hinges, and I ran in, very fast, the bright light inside blinding me.

His back was to me; he was firing a burst from his Schmeisser through the serving hatch. Then he was swinging the gun to face the new danger behind him, trying at the same time to assure himself that the broken bottle and the gentle blue flames did not mean something far more lethal; it was just too much for him to cope with all at once, and the swathe of his bullets cut an arc as they splattered into the walls. I heard the window shatter, and then he was round to face me. I used my foot, the quickest weapon a man has. I brought my right leg up, swung my body over to the left, aimed at the hand that was round the stock; the finger on the trigger, and kicked hard, very hard. He went sprawling across the room, and the gun went flying from his hand, and I had my foot on it as he lay there, staring up at me in what can only be described as utter disbelief.

I said: "Don't move, Cernik. Don't even move a muscle."

The gentle blue flame of the cognac was playing around his feet, and he stared at me, not believing. He wore dark blue trousers and high leather boots, a black sweater and a black beret, and his face was blackened too, a shadow crawling through the darkness of the night, the skilled night fighter at work, invisible. And sentries outside, back and front, not even knowing he was there.

I thought of the dossier we had compiled, the brilliant soldier who got through all his classes in record time, the highest honors. I have the highest respect for competence, but this wasn't the time to reflect on it.

I said: "Flat on your back, both hands behind your head." He did as he was told, quite slowly, and I took one of the sheepskin chair covers, tossed it over his head and said: "Leave it there, and don't move an inch."

I could afford to take my eyes off him now. I saw Krnj at the serving hatch, staring in, and I put a finger to my lips and made a signal: come on in. He nodded and disappeared.

Fenrek was lying on his back on the floor, his wrists so tightly bound that they were bleeding, his ankles tied too; worse, there was a quarter-inch nylon cord around his forehead, a stick twisting it tight. I loosened it quickly; he was out cold; I wondered if his skull was cracked.

Agathon was lying in a corner, huddled up on his side, his knees in his stomach, and there was blood on the floor beneath him. The blue flames were mixing with the blood, and they were going out now. I turned him over with my foot. He was still alive, but the blood was seeping out of a long, deep cut across his belly, the Bulgar's terrible stomach wound that kills, but infinitely slowly, and with agonizing pain. He was groaning softly, and his swarthy face was white as an aspirin.

The whimper was hoarse: "I'm dying, Cain. Dying."

"I know it."

Under the sheepskin covering his face, Cernik had not stirred. I found my pocketknife and cut the cords that were binding Fenrek, and then Krnj was there. He'd found the sentry's gun and was holding it on Cernik, the safety catch off, taking in the situation. He said: "May I?" Without waiting for a reply, he leaned down and pulled the sheep-skin away, looked at Cernik and nodded slowly, almost to himself. He said: "So you were right."

"Of course."

He broke wind loudly, very loudly, and I said: "Get Fenrek up to where the others are. I'll follow you."

He did not take his eyes off Cernik. He said: "There may be fifty of them pouring into the house at any minute now."

"I know. So you'd better hurry."

"Be careful, Cain. He's the most dangerous of them all."

"I know that too. Go now."

"All right." He put down his rifle, very carefully, dropped to one knee and hoisted Fenrek over his shoulder in a fireman's lift. His eyes were on Cernik all the time, and he was smiling quite genially, as though inviting him to make a sudden move. A stray bullet smashed through the broken windows and thumped into the drapes, and he said again: "They may be here soon now."

"I'll be right behind you."

When he had gone, I found a corner where I could watch both entrances, and held the Degtyrarov ready, and Cernik, very slowly, sat up, quite cool and in control now, and when I did not shoot him dead there and then, he got just as carefully to his feet, and I said: "All right, now that you're comfortable, not anymore."

His face was hard as a barrel full of shrapnel, his eyes wary, his mouth firmly set. He said: "I prefer to die on my feet. You are Cain, aren't you? You could hardly be anyone else. I'm Klaus Cernik, but you know that."

I knew that I was seeking for comfort, rather than making one last effort to be absolutely sure; but I had to say it. I knew that it was desperation, nothing else, that I was asking a question to which I already knew the answer, that there was not the remotest likelihood... But I *had* to ask it, none the less.

It did not sound like my own voice: "Did you kill Helen

Poulardis?"

He answered me, quite clearly, before he spoke. The reflex was not as clear as Agathon's had been, but that last wisp of hope had gone. No surprise, no feigned emotion, why should there be? He raised his shoulders and said:

"No, I didn't. If she's dead, it was almost certainly Gravena. A painted whore, why should I be interested in Helen Poulardis? Where's my wife?"

I did not answer him. I wondered why she'd never given her numbers to him before, when they were together. But I thought I knew the answer to that too; in the old days, she hadn't been that kind of a woman, she was more *his* kind of a woman. But now, for her the times had changed, and there was all that money for just the two of them. Couldn't she even have guessed that he'd be hunting her down, like an animal?

The moaning in the corner had almost stopped. The blue flames creeping softly along the floor had expired. Agathon gave a last shuddering gasp, and there was silence.

Cernik said again: "Where's my wife? I've got a score to settle with her, a very personal score."

I jerked my head at the body in the corner: "Agathon, did you get the rest of the digits from him?"

"Of course." He snorted, and said: "He never had any stamina, not really. They executed him once, did you know that? Only they killed the wrong man. An escape like that makes a man want to hang on to life, and for the Agathons of this world, that's a perilous situation to be in. He was number one, once, did you know that? And now...now look at him."

I said: "All over for him, and for you too, Cernik."

He was terribly cool and self-possessed. He said carelessly: "We could share it, you know. Ten million dollars is a lot of money."

"And the revolution?"

He laughed: "For God's sake! All that rubbish was Agathon's idea, not mine. Sure, in the old days I was one of them, I was a fanatic then. But too many prisons, Cain, it makes a man long for better things. I won't offer you half, but...a million or two?"

"You are understating your own intelligence."

He shrugged: "I thought it might be worth a try. My men will break through the defenses pretty soon, and then where will you be?"

I said: "Gone. Move. And move very carefully."

I gestured towards the door with the Degtyrarov, and he smiled and said: "Very well."

It was the smile, of course, that was the mistake. He was overplaying the hand, they always do.

He moved like greased lightning, leaping at me so fast that I was barely conscious of the movement. I felt his hands on the machine gun, one powerful grip on the barrel, the other on the stock, his arms outthrust and ramming into me, stiff as steel rods. I raised my hands up high as I went over backwards, dropping quickly to the ground, and he let go the gun with his right hand and had a knife there, a long, thin-bladed knife which came out of the top of his boot with bewildering speed. I saw it go up, and in his eyes there was a cold, calculating and quite dispassionate awareness of what he had to do and how he had to do it; the precision of a Theseus killing the Minotaur. But this was no Theseus, no Greek, he came from over the border, in Bulgaria, where the Anastenarides came from...

I was on my back, rolling over fast, and my right foot was planted firmly in his stomach, and for a moment he was poised there, for all the world like one of the ancient Minoans who somersaulted so lithely over the horns of the charging bulls. I let go of everything, threw out my arms, and straightened my leg, hard and fast and furious. The gun, the knife, and Cernik went flying, hurtling across the room like cannonballs. I heard him smash into the wall, high up near the ceiling, and I was on my feet again and ready before he hit the ground.

His head rolled loosely to one side when I touched it; his neck was broken, and he was dead.

I switched out the lights, waited for a moment, listening to the sound of the gunfire—was it growing less now?—and ran fast, very fast, up the mountainside towards Athene's *hestia,* to the bubbling spring where her tears were still, after so many centuries, coming out of the hot and angry earth.

CHAPTER 13

The savagery of the gunfire had all gone.

Now, there were just one or two sporadic bursts, a few isolated shots, the occasional *crummmppp* of a mortar. Some of them, no doubt, would have reached the villa by now, the attackers crashing in or the defenders withdrawing, the winners and the losers both finding their leaders dead and all their scheming come to nothing.

I didn't think it mattered very much who was winning, or who was losing; the battle was almost over, and the prize had been lost, forever. Ten million dollars would just sit there, the interest piling up, for another how many years? Would it *ever* come to light? I didn't see how it could.

I was moving slowly now, creeping in downwind; on the faint breeze I could hear her sobbing quietly. I heard Tsamados' husky voice, a whisper carried on a zephyr: "Just hang on, they'll be here soon, I know they will."

Another burst of gunfire far away to the left, and then silence again. The night was cold, the air crisp, the white moon coming up over the mountain now. I walked in quietly, and Tsamados spun round, ready to fight, his whole body tensed.

He saw it was me, and dropped to the ground again, close beside her, and said, whispering: "She's hurt, badly hurt"

He'd pulled her dress open at the breast, cold as alabaster in the pale moonlight, and was daubing at the blood there, trying to staunch its flow. He looked at me helplessly and said: "We walked into a burst of gunfire, almost here, and...and this had to happen. Where's Colonel Fenrek, for God's sake?"

"Krnj is bringing him. Soon now."

Maria's eyes were closed, but now she opened them and looked up at me, the fear still there. The night was so silent you could hear the faint rustling of the pine needles. A frog began to croak nearby. There was a small black hole under her left breast, a little to the side. I tore the rest of her dress away, and ran my fingers over her, searching for an exit wound; nothing; the bullet was still in there, inside the rib cage, close to her heart. There was dark blue blood, lung blood, at her lips, and I took Tsamados' handkerchief and wiped it gently away.

She whispered: "Mat? Mat Fenrek?"

"He'll be here soon. Don't talk."

"I have to."

I looked at Tsamados. "Go down the slope and see if you can find Krnj, he may need help, it's a long way."

"All right." He began to hobble off, clutching his pudgy thigh, and I said: "Are you hurt?" A foolish question, it was obvious that he was. He said: "It's nothing, in one side and out the other." Painfully, he moved away.

She was crying very quietly now. She whispered: "You know, don't you?"

"Yes. I know. Don't talk about it."

"Does Fenrek?"

"No."

"Will he? Ever?"

"Not from me."

"Will you promise me that?"

"Yes. I promise." I took a long, deep breath; the shuddering was coming on again. "Why did you have to kill Helen? She couldn't have harmed you? Why did you have to..." My voice trailed off.

She turned her face to one side, choking, and I wiped away the blood again. She said: "I didn't think...I didn't think you'd find out from her...what she'd done with...with the money. I thought you'd be...too gentle. I needed that money, from the robbery...the bank.

"For your husband?"

"Yes. For Klaus. I learned she'd given you the key, and...she knew who I was. I didn't expect that. Just...chance." She turned back and looked up at me, her eyes filled with pain. Her voice was so quiet I could hardly hear it. "Twenty years ago, when the fund was transferred...it was I who arranged it. They needed someone who wasn't...in hiding. I'd been with them...earlier, and Helen was one of the children we had taken over the border into Bulgaria. She remembered me, and so...I had to... How did you find out?"

Chance, chance, all the time, the wheel always turning; the Greeks have a better word for it.

I said: "We found out about Helen because she used a bill that happened to have a special mark on it, a noticeable mark, remember? It's ironic. I found out about you because you did precisely the same thing. I left money for Helen, and then you paid a taxi driver with a bill that I'd seen before. A lot of other, little things, but that clinched it. You were lucky that Agathon himself never saw you, he'd have killed you a long time ago."

"Lucky?" The irony was hers now, twisted.

I said: "And all this time, is that why you and Fenrek..."

She interrupted me, fiercely, and winced with the pain of her vehemence. "No! No, no, no! It was only when he started looking for Agathon that I realized...if I could find Agathon I could get the money. For Klaus. We'd all thought for so long that Agathon was dead, that the money was lost forever."

If she'd found Agathon! The things he would have done to her!

She said: "I was so...so..."

"Confused?" I tried to be gentle with her. Her suffering had been going on for a long time. It's not the body that hurts, ever; it's always the heart.

She turned her face to one side, her breath rasping now, and then looked back at me, more anguished and weary than ever: "You never told Fenrek?"

"And I never will. He's my friend."

"And so...so was I."

"You still are, Maria. He loves you very dearly."

"Yes, I know that. Is he all right?"

"Yes."

She tried to pull her dress up over her breasts, and I took off my jacket and covered her. She said, forcing herself: "Can you believe...a woman can love two people at once? Deeply?"

"Yes."

"When Klaus broke out of jail, I knew...I knew that I had to go back to him. And yet, I couldn't bring myself to...leave Fenrek. They love me too, both of them."

I said: "No, not Cernik. He had a score to settle with you, that's all."

Her eyes had been quieter; now they were troubled again. She said: "No, no, you're wrong! He must have broken out when..." She was gasping for breath now, and I said again:

"Don't talk, there's nothing more to tell."

"I must, I must! He broke out when...he heard about Stefan Crespos."

"No. He must have learned of that a lot earlier. That sort of thing gets round the prisons very quickly. The likelihood is that he broke out when he heard about you and Fenrek. That was the score he had to settle, his wife finally taking up with another man while he was behind bars. That sort of news wouldn't filter through to him quite so easily, but when it did..."

"Oh, my God..."

Even now she didn't ask about Cernik. I could sense her bewilderment, her confusion, her pain. How long had she been trying to choose between them? How long had she been tormenting herself? She was coughing now, and I held her tight and said: "Easy, easy, he'll be here soon."

"And he's...all right?"

"Yes, he is fine." Now was the time to tell her. "And Cernik is dead."

She did not whimper. She sighed and said: "I felt that, I felt that perhaps he was."

I took her hand, ice-cold, in mine and sat beside her and waited, and she looked at me and then turned her head away and closed her eyes.

* * *

They came, at last, the three of them. Tsamados was limping horribly now, and Krnj and Fenrek were supporting him. Fenrek's face was drawn and pale, and there was still the dark stain around his wrists; but there was worse for him to come.

He looked at me, his eyes terribly weary, and then he dropped to where Maria was lying; I had covered her face with the jacket, and he knelt down beside her quickly and lifted it, and looked at her for a long, long time.

He said nothing. He put the jacket back gently, and sat there on the ground beside her, his knees drawn up, his arms around his long legs; he stared at the ground in front of him and was silent.

I said at last: "A bullet from one of them. One side or the other." He did not answer me.

Krnj took Tsamados' arm and said: "Why don't we start on down to the village?" Tsamados looked at me, and I nodded, and they moved off slowly together under the moon and through the trees, and I stood there and waited for Fenrek to speak.

In a little while, he said, still staring into the ground, speaking very quietly: "I know what you think about my...amours, Cain. Yes, there are many beautiful women, very many. Only this one... I would have married Maria, can you believe that? Only...she had a husband somewhere still. Three dead and one still living, did you know that?"

I shook my head: "No. I didn't know."

"I don't know who he was, anything about him. Sometimes, I tried to talk to her, only it always pained her to speak of him, and... The Anastenarides don't have divorce, so we just...let it drag along." He said again, that terrible weariness heavy on him: "We would have been married. And like this... Right at the end." He looked up at me and said: "It *is* over, isn't it? Krnj told me."

"Yes, Cernik and Agathon, both dead. The money—some Swiss bank a little richer."

He put out a hand and laid it on Maria's body, as though trying to feed some life back into her. He said: "A wonderful, wonderful woman." I let him talk, let him seek the comfort. "Three years now, we've been together, ever since... Did you know she passed all her courses with honors? In record time." They both had, I reflected, the two of them. "She would have gone a long way in the Department, a very long way, and now..."

"We must get her back to her family. Do you know them?"

He shook his head. "No family. Just a young nephew, he works in my Department in Paris."

There'd be time later to find out his name. A discreet hint to retire, that's all that would be needed.

I said: "Then we should take her down to Athens, her home."

"Yes."

"I'll carry her down to the village."

"No. I'd like to do that myself."

"You're all right now?"

"Physically, yes."

"All right."

The moon was higher now, whiter than ever, bathing the valley in pale beauty; the dark trees, undulating down the hillsides, were almost black, mile upon mile of olive and fir, cascading down to the sea.

He said: "And you? What will you do now?"

"I'm going back to Serigrad. Just for a while."

"To Serigrad?"

"Someone I would like to see there."

Absently, he nodded. He picked Maria's body up gently in his arms, and moved off with her over the ancient, broken stones, the stones that had known Athene, and Artemis, and Persephone, and Aphrodite, and Callisto, the most beautiful of them all.

I followed a little way behind him.

The bubbling sound of the spring was cool, and fresh, and cleansing, the tears that Athene had left behind her. The damp mist was rising, the clouds over the mountain. Somewhere, an owl was hooting.

And all the rest was silence.

THE END

ABOUT THE AUTHOR

Alan Lyle-Smythe was born in Surrey, England. Prior to World War II, he served with the Palestine Police from 1936 to 1939 and learned the Arabic language. He was awarded an MBE in June 1938. He married Aliza Sverdova in 1939, then studied acting from 1939 to 1941.

In January 1940, Lyle-Smythe was commissioned in the Royal Army Service Corps. Due to his linguistic skills, he transferred to the Intelligence Corps and served in the Western Desert, in which he used the surname "Caillou" (the French word for 'pebble') as an alias.

He was captured in North Africa, imprisoned and threatened with execution in Italy, then escaped to join the British forces at Salerno. He was then posted to serve with the partisans in Yugoslavia. He wrote about his experiences in the book *The World is Six Feet Square* (1954). He was promoted to captain and awarded the Military Cross in 1944.

Following the war, he returned to the Palestine Police from 1946 to 1947, then served as a Police Commissioner in British-occupied Italian Somaliland from 1947 to 1952, where he was recommissioned a captain.

After work as a District Officer in Somalia and professional hunter, Lyle-Smythe travelled to Canada, where he worked as a hunter and then became an actor on Canadian television.

He wrote his first novel, *Rogue's Gambit*, in 1955, first using the name Caillou, one of his aliases from the war. Moving from Vancouver to Hollywood, he made an appearance as a contestant on the January 23 1958 edition of *You Bet Your Life*.

He appeared as an actor and/or worked as a screenwriter in such shows as *Daktari*, *The Man From U.N.C.L.E.* (including the screenwriting for "*The Bow-Wow Affair*" from 1965), *Thriller*, *Daniel Boone*, *Quark*, *Centennial*, and *How the West Was Won*. In 1966-67, he had a recurring role (as Jason Flood) in NBC's "*Tarzan*" TV series starring Ron Ely. Caillou appeared in such television movies as *Sole Survivor* (1970), *The Hound of the Baskervilles* (1972, as Inspector Lestrade), and *Goliath Awaits* (1981). His cinema film credits included roles in *Five Weeks in a Balloon* (1962), *Clarence, the Cross-Eyed Lion* (1965), *The Rare Breed* (1966), *The Devil's Brigade* (1968), *Hellfighters* (1968), *Everything You Always Wanted to Know About Sex* (*But Were Afraid to Ask)* (1972), *Herbie Goes to Monte Carlo* (1977), *Beyond Evil* (1980), *The Sword and the Sorcerer* (1982) and *The Ice Pirates* (1984).

Caillou wrote 52 paperback thrillers under his own name and the nom de plume of Alex Webb, with such heroes as Cabot Cain, Colonel Matthew Tobin, Mike Benasque, Ian Quayle and Josh Dekker, as well as writing many magazine stories.

Several of Caillou's novels were made into films, such as *Rampage* with Robert Mitchum in 1963, based on his big game hunting knowledge; *Assault on Agathon*, for which Caillou did the screenplay as well; and *The Cheetahs*, filmed in 1989.

He was married to Aliza Sverdova from 1939 until his death. Their daughter Nadia Caillou was the screenwriter for the film *Skeleton Coast*.

Alan Caillou died in Sedona, Arizona in 2006.

DON'T MISS ANY OF NEIL HUNTER'S NOVELS FROM CALIBER BOOKS

Reporter Les Mason is completing an expose on the Long Point Nuclear Plant. But before he can finish he dies an agonizing death. The doctors are baffled—and there are similar cases to follow...Chris Lane, his girlfriend, and organizer of the Long Point Protestors, discovers Mason's notes, and decides to find out for herself what the plant has to hide.

2 BOOK SERIES

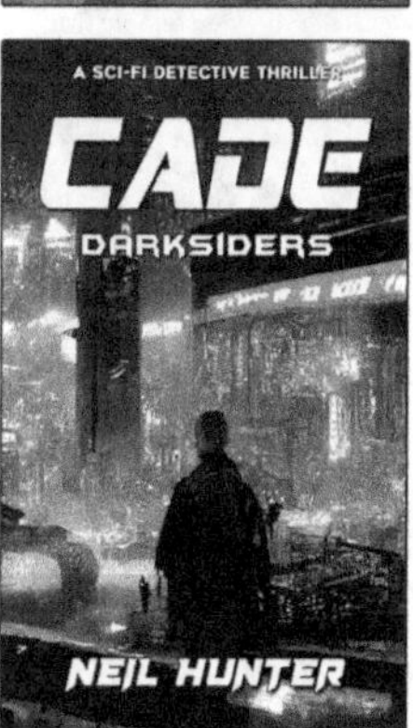

In middle of the 21st century America – over-populated decaying cities are ruled by hi-tech gangs pushing every vice and wastelands are controlled by bands of mutants. Ordinary citizens are oppressed and face a hopeless future. But Marshal T.J. Cade is a new breed of law enforcer. Teamed with his cyborg partner, Janek, Cade takes on these criminals and works in the gray areas of the law to get the job done.

3 BOOK SERIES

The village of Shepthorne England wasn't being gripped, but strangled by a winter's blanket of heavy snow and Arctic temperatures. The trouble began innocently enough with a massive pile-up of autos on frozen roads leading to and from the village. Then, from the sky, a military transport plane with its top secret cargo of devastation crashed down towards the center of the village. Hell was just beginning to touch Shepthorne and its unsuspecting citizens...

FROM CALIBER BOOKS

www.calibercomics.com

CALIBER COMICS GOES TO WAR!
HISTORICAL AND MILITARY THEMED GRAPHIC NOVELS

WORLD WAR ONE:
MO MAN'S LAND
ISBN: 9781635298123

A look at World War 1 from the French trenches as they faced the Imperial German Army.

CORTEZ AND THE FALL OF THE AZTECS
ISBN: 9781635299779

Cortez battles the Aztecs while in search of Inca gold.

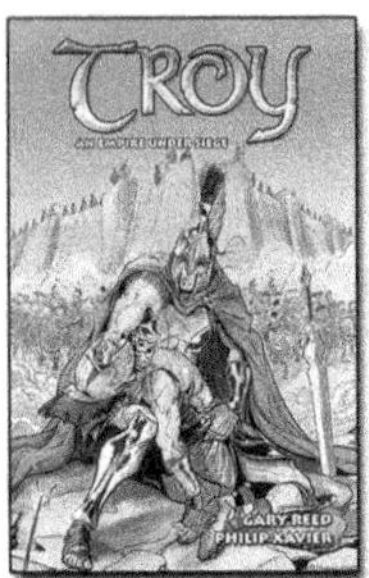

TROY:
AN EMPIRE UNDER SIEGE
ISBN: 9781635298635

Homer's famous The Iliad and the Trojan War is given a unique human perspective rather than from the God's.

WITNESS TO WAR
ISBN: 9781635299700

WW2's Battle of the Bulge is seen up close by an embedded female war reporter.

THE LINCOLN BRIGADE
ISBN: 9781635298222

American volunteers head to Spain in the 1930s to fight in their civil war against the fascist regime.

EL CID:
THE CONQUEROR
ISBN: 9780982654996

Europe's greatest warrior attempts to unify Spain against invading foreign and domestic armies.

WINTER WAR
ISBN: 9780985749392

At the outbreak of WW2 Finland fights against an invading Soviet army.

ZULUNATION:
END OF EMPIRE
ISBN: 9780941613415

The global British Empire and far-reaching influence is threatened by a Zulu uprising in southern Africa.

AIR WARRIORS: WORLD WAR ONE #V1 - V4
Take to the skys of WW1 as various fighter aces tell their harrowing stories.

ISBN: 9781635297973 (V1), 9781635297980 (V2), 9781635297997 (V3), 9781635298000 (V4)

CALIBER COMICS PRESENTS
The Complete
VIETNAM JOURNAL

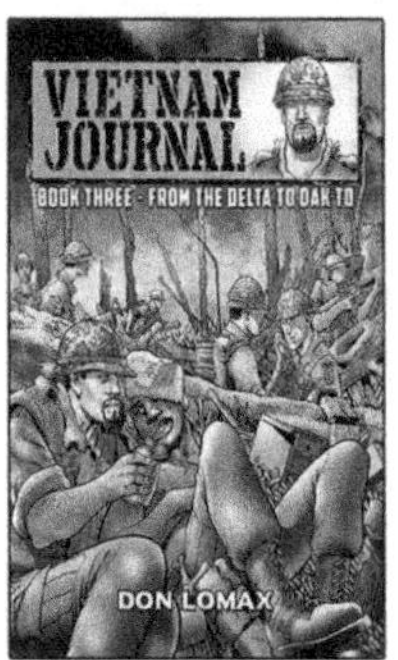
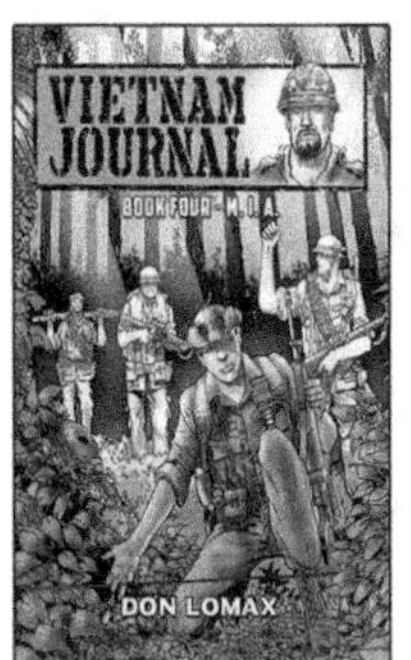

8 Volumes Covering the Entire Initial Run of the Critically Acclaimed Don Lomax Series

And Now Available
VIETNAM JOURNAL SERIES TWO
"INCURSION", "JOURNEY INTO HELL", "RIPCORD"

All new stories from Scott 'Journal' Neithammer as he reports durings the later stages of the Vietnam War.

CALIBER COMICS   WWW.CALIBERCOMICS.COM

ALSO AVAILABLE FROM DON LOMAX

HIGH SHINING BRASS

High Shining Brass is based on the true story of an American spy during the Vietnam War as told to Don Lomax by agent Robert Durand who chronicles the tale. Durand was a member of a black-ops team, code- named "Shining Brass." The series depicts the horrific atrocities witnessed and performed by the once naïve special forces member as he attempts to perform his duties and understand the true meaning behind the madness. Durand's group was under the command of a combined force, comprised of every branch of the services, and headed up by the ever-popular Central Intelligence Committee. It's a journey into a shadow world of treachery and deceit—and reveals the way lives of Americans were traded about carelessly during the war in Vietnam.

ISBN: 978-1544962191 $14.99US

ABOVE AND BEYOND

Beginning in May of 2007, noted comic writer and illustrator Don Lomax teamed up with Police and Security News magazine to produce the series "Above and Beyond" - real life depictions of heroic acts by law enforcement professionals. Just as our soldiers here and abroad deserve recognition for their unwavering service, so do the men and women who protect and serve the citizens of the United States. Contained within these pages are just a few stories of these individuals who have demonstrated selfless bravery and heroic action under the most difficult circumstances and gone above and beyond the call of duty.

ISBN: 978-1635299601 $ 9.99 US

WWW.CALIBERCOMICS.COM

ALSO AVAILABLE FROM DON LOMAX

FIRE TEAM

Cam Ky MacMurphy is half-Vietnamese, half-American, and feels as if he doesn't belong to either race. His uncle, Nguyen Van Tan, raised him from birth and the two live in an area of town that is controlled by a skinhead gang. The neighborhood lives in fear as the gang forces them to pay "protection" money. Then hope appears in the form of a ghost from the past. When Nguyen was young he worked with a U.S. Fire Team deployed in the twilight days of the Vietnam War. The team ended up sacrificing their lives while trying to evacuate women and children from an overrun base. Now the Fire Team has come back from the dead to not only save Nguyen and Cam but bring news to Cam that his American father is alive and fighting a guerrilla war in the Vietnamese jungles!

ISBN: 978-1635297812 $16.99US

THE BOYS IN THE BASEMENT

For those that enjoy the world of model railroading! THE BOYS IN THE BASEMENT cartoon strip was conceived, written, and illustrated by award-winning comic book creator Don Lomax. Don made a career of working in the train industry before and after serving his country with a tour in Vietnam. Don takes a humorous look at the world of model trains from the perspective of three men, Merle and his friends Lenny and Earl, and their obsession and love with the hobby. As they attempt to build the perfect model railroad layout in Merle's basement.

ISBN: 978-1635298031 $ 12.99 US

WWW.CALIBERCOMICS.COM

ALSO AVAILABLE FROM CALIBER COMICS

QUALITY GRAPHIC NOVELS TO ENTERTAIN

THE SEARCHERS: VOLUME 1
The Shape of Things to Come

Before *League of Extraordinary Gentlemen* there was *The Searchers*. At the dawn of the 20th Century the greatest literary adventurers from the minds of Wells, Doyle, Burroughs, and Haggard were created. All thought to be the work of pure fiction. However, a century later, the real-life descendents of those famous characters are recuited by the legendary Professor Challenger in order to save mankind's future. Series collected for the first time.

"Searchers is the comic book I have on the wall with a sign reading · 'Love books? Never read a comic? Try this one! ….money back guarantee…" - Dark Star Books.

WAR OF THE WORLDS: INFESTATION

Based on the H.G. Wells classic! The "Martian Invasion" has begun again and now mankind must fight for its very humanity. It happened slowly at first but by the third year, it seemed that the war was almost over… the war was almost lost.

"Writer Randy Zimmerman has a fine grasp of drama, and spins the various strands of the story into a coherent whole… imaginative and very gritty."
- war-of-the-worlds.co.uk

HELSING: LEGACY BORN

From writer Gary Reed (Deadworld) and artists John Lowe (Captain America), Bruce McCorkindale (Godzilla). She was born into a legacy she wanted no part of and pushed into a battle recessed deep in the shadows of the night. Samantha Helsing is torn between two worlds…two allegiances…two families. The legacy of the Van Helsing family and their crusade against the "night creatures" comes to modern day with the most unlikely of all warriors.

"Congratulations on this masterpiece…"
- Paul Dale Roberts, Compuserve Reviews

DEADWORLD

Before there was The Walking Dead there was Deadworld. Here is an introduction of the long running classic horror series, Deadworld, to a new audience! Considered by many to be the godfather of the original zombie comic with over 100 issues and graphic novels in print and over 1,000,000 copies sold, Deadworld ripped into the undead with intelligent zombies on a mission and a group of poor teens riding in a school bus desperately try to stay one step ahead of the sadistic, Harley-riding King Zombie. Death, mayhem, and a touch of supernatural evil made Deadworld a classic and now here's your chance to get into the story!

DAYS OF WRATH

Award winning comic writer & artist Wayne Vansant brings his gripping World War II saga of war in the Pacific to Guadalcanal and the Battle of Bloody Ridge. This is the powerful story of the long, vicious battle for Guadalcanal that occurred in 1942-43. When the U.S. Navy orders its outnumbered and out-gunned ships to run from the Japanese fleet, they abandon American troops on a bloody, battered island in the South Pacific.

"Heavy on authenticity, compellingly written and beautifully drawn."
- Comics Buyers Guide

SHERLOCK HOLMES:
THE CASE OF THE MISSING MARTIAN

Sherlock is called out of retirement to London in 1908 to solve a most baffling mystery: The British Museum is missing a specimen of a Martian from the failed invasion of 1899. Did it walk away on its own or did someone steal it?

Holmes ponders the facts and remembers his part in the war effort alongside Professor Challenger during the War of the Worlds invasion that was chronicled in H.G. Wells' classic novel.

Meanwhile, Doctor Watson has problems of his own when his wife steals a scalpel from his surgical tool kit and returns to her old stomping grounds of Whitechapel, the London

CALIBER PRESENTS

The original Caliber Presents anthology title was one of Caliber's inaugural releases and featured predominantly new creators, many of which went onto successful careers in the comics' industry. In this new version, Caliber Presents has expanded to graphic novel size and while still featuring new creators it also includes many established professional creators with new visions. Creators featured in this first issue include nominees and winners of some of the industry's major awards including the Eisner, Harvey, Xeric, Ghastly, Shel Dorf, Comic Monsters, and more.

LEGENDLORE

From Caliber Comics now comes the entire Realm and Legendlore saga as a set of volumes that collects the long running critically acclaimed series. In the vein of The Lord of The Rings and The Hobbit with elements of Game of Thrones and Dungeon and Dragons.

Four normal modern day teenagers are plunged into a world they thought only existed in novels and film. They are whisked away to a magical land where dragons roam the skies, orcs and hobgoblins terrorize travelers, where unicorns prance through the forest, and kingdoms wage war for dominance. It is a world where man is just one race, joining other races such as elves, trolls, dwarves, changelings, and the dreaded night creatures who steal the night.

TIME GRUNTS

What if Hitler's last great Super Weapon was – Time itself! A WWII/time travel adventure that can best be described as *Band of Brothers* meets *Time Bandits*.

October, 1944. Nazi fortunes appear bleaker by the day. But in the bowels of the Wenceslas Mines, a terrible threat has emerged . . . The Nazis have discovered the ability to conquer time itself with the help of a new ominous device!

Now a rag tag group of American GIs must stop this threat to the past, present, and future . . . While dealing with their own past, prejudices, and fears in the process.

CALIBER
COMICS

www.calibercomics.com